Clifton Johnson

A Book of Country Clouds and Sunshine

Clifton Johnson

A Book of Country Clouds and Sunshine

ISBN/EAN: 9783337227708

Printed in Europe, USA, Canada, Australia, Japan

Cover: Foto ©Andreas Hilbeck / pixelio.de

More available books at **www.hansebooks.com**

A BOOK OF COUNTRY CLOUDS AND SUNSHINE

TEXT AND ILLUSTRATIONS
BY CLIFTON JOHNSON

BOSTON LEE AND SHEPARD
PUBLISHERS MDCCCXCVII

CONTENTS

LIST OF ILLUSTRATIONS

INTRODUCTION

THE "Clouds and Sunshine" which make up this book are those of life rather than those of nature. The book is, first of all, about the farmer and his ways, about village life and character. What country life really is, I have tried to make clear, with the use of rose-colored spectacles. On the other hand, I have no wish to lay undue stress on the shadows. Country life has its drawbacks; yet, to my feeling, a pleasant New England village, not too far removed from a large town and the railroad, is the best dwelling-place in the world. New England has a charm of variety that few other regions of our country can rival. It has a virile individuality that its own children can never forget. One grows to love its rough hills and wooded mountain ridges, the singing of its streams, its summer heats, its winter storms, even; and no amount of prosperity and honor elsewhere can entirely compensate for this loss.

I spoke of a country village as being the ideal home. You cannot, however, get its aroma and its finer pleasures by moving into such a village, — not even if you build a mansion there. You must yourself be simple, must do without the mansion, and love a home of humble comfort better, must live the country life. Pride or style or artificiality will never get at the heart of that life, and will miss much of the country sweetness.

The chapters, "Winter Life in New England," and "The Farm Day by Day," were first published in *The Outlook;* "How Spring Comes," and "A Hill-Town Sabbath," appeared in *The Congregationalist;* "Deserted Homes" appeared in *The Cosmopolitan Magazine.*

I.

WINTER LIFE IN NEW ENGLAND

WHAT the New England summer is, many visitors from the outside world well know. Very few outsiders, however, know by experience very much about the New England winter. Rarely, too, has it been pictured, except somewhat romantically from the artist's imagination or memory. Yet it is to be doubted if at any season New England is more beautiful. The contour of every hill and mountain slope lies exposed, and at no other time can one so clearly comprehend the real nature of the country. Everywhere is the wide expanse of the snow, broken at frequent intervals by patches of woodland with their gray masses of tree-trunks, and their bare twigs making a delicate tracery against the sky. In the outlooks from the highlands, or across the wide valleys, the landscape melts in the distance into mellow blues, and the tints of the winter skies are of unequalled brilliance; while at night the stars glitter and sparkle through an air of crystalline charms.

Then there are mornings when the frost takes possession of the land, and every tree-twig and every sprig of grass that shows above the snow has a white coating. The sun shines on a world

of dreams, and I doubt if any tropic land could rival the enchant-
ment and radiance of such a morning.

Often the higher ridges of the hills are crowned with the
solemn green masses of a pine or spruce wood, as dark and stiff

WINTER AMONG THE HILLS

as nearly all the rest of the world is light and delicate.   In places
the rocks lift dark shoulders to break the whiteness; and along
the roads, where habitations are near, are black lines of stone
wall.   Then there are the frequent weather-beaten and unpainted
old houses and out-buildings, that emphasize by their gray gloom
the light tones which are general.   This type of house is most
often found in the lonely outlying districts.   In the villages
nearly all the houses are painted white.   It makes an odd impression to come on a little village of white houses in this winter world.   They differ so slightly from the surrounding snowfields

that the impression is quite ghostly. To look down on some wide expanse of country from a hilltop, and see it all given over to the drifted snows, gives the feeling that only a miracle can ever bring back the greens of spring and summer. Among the tumbled ridges of the hills the occasional lonely little farms seem entirely lost, and the forsakenness of the region is appalling.

I suppose the majority of New Englanders take winter as a matter of course; and yet I have been told by a Yankee, who gathered his wisdom by years of experience as a peddler, that many of them wasted half their lives in wishing it was not such abominably cold weather.

When, in autumn, the fields turn brown, and the leaves fall, and the frosty nights begin to hint at the coming cold, few look forward to the approaching winter with feelings of pleasure. The thought of it brings a shiver; and the imagined delight of a trip South, or to California, pictures itself in many minds. But such trips belong to the realm of the impossible, though I do know of a single case where a man of moderate means has one farm among the Massachusetts hills and another in Florida. To the latter the farmer and his wife go each year at the approach of cold weather, and return in the spring. When they leave the one place or the other they find some one who is willing to live on the vacant farm, and look after it in consideration of a free rental. But very likely this man is the only one of his kind in all New England.

A great many people prepare for winter by banking up their houses with leaves or cornstalks held in place by boards staked against them. Some use sods for this banking. On the most exposed sides of the house double windows are fastened, and storm-doors are put on at the main entrances. There is a general search for cracks to be stopped, and a good deal of tinkering is done about the out-buildings to make things snug for the hens and cattle.

As far as the cold is concerned, winter is most disturbing in

the shiver awakened by its approach. Mentally and constitution-
ally one soon gets adjusted to it, and finds the winter occupations,

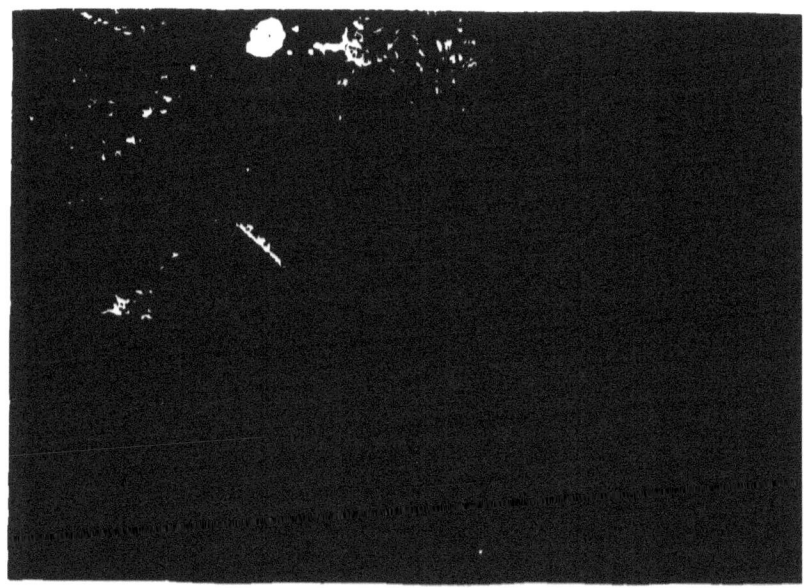

AN EARLY SNOW

the crisp air and the brilliant sunshine, or the white whirl of the
storms, in many ways enjoyable. Besides, it no sooner settles
down to really cold weather than we begin to look forward to
spring, and that gives a warmth which nothing else can.

A New Englander who has attained distinction in his particular calling has sometimes told me that when he and his
brothers were little fellows, and slept in the room under the roof
in the L, the snows would sift in at the cracks in the winter
storms ; and when they ran down stairs in the morning, they left
behind them the tracks of their bare feet in the little drifts.
Such stories seem by right to belong to the days of the first

settlers ; but when you drive along the crooked New England roadways next summer, notice the houses. There are some, yes, a good many, which seem not to have been shingled for an age. The shingles curl up with brittle decay, and in places have dropped away altogether. Such a roof every storm must penetrate. Notice the windows of the more shabby houses. You can count many broken panes. Some are stuffed out with rags or an old hat. Some have been stopped with shingles or boards nailed on. Some are not stopped at all. In the heavier rains, there are probably pots and pans set about under the leaks. In winter, there is a cleaning up after each snowstorm. I do not mean that such houses are the rule, but only that such do exist in greater numbers than the casual observer would suspect. The typical house of the New England country is the white-painted building of a story and a half or two stories, with green blinds, and a piazza, and possibly a bay-window. It is kept in fair repair, and in ordinary weather is quite comfortable.

Perhaps the hardest thing the inhabitants have to do in a New England winter is to get up in the morning. The air of the sleeping-rooms is almost as keen as that of outdoors. The window-panes are blurred with frost. Every breath of the sleepers makes a visible cloud of vapor. The bed is comfortable enough. The feather-bed, beneath, half envelops one, and above are blanket after blanket, and quilt on quilt. Jack Frost would have to be a much sharper fellow than he is to penetrate that mass. But to make up one's mind to step out from this warm nest is a serious matter. The older members of the family get up from a sense of responsibility and the force of habit. The younger members get up in response to calls from the foot of the stairs, because they have to.

In towns near railroads the majority of farmers burn coal in the sitting-room stove, and the fire is kept going all winter. The man who depends on wood usually has a sitting-room stove large enough to hold some very sizable "chunks ;" and these knotty lumps of unsplitable wood, put in the last thing in the evening, are still burning the next morning. Yet the fire is very apt to burn low by the time Mr. Farmer arises, and he finds the kitchen, at least, full of cold ; and we can imagine him moving shiveringly about there until he has the fire started. It may be it is Mrs. Farmer who kindles the fire, and has to shiver in the cold kitchen ; but we will give Mr. Farmer the credit for being more gallant than to allow that, usually.

During the coldest weather it is no easy matter to keep the house warm, even in the daytime; and in spite of the old overcoats laid down to keep the sharp outer air from entering under the doors, the wind and the frost are persistent, and they come in at every crack ; and some of the houses are so decrepit with age, or lack of care, that it would be no wonder if at times the inmates

COLD WEATHER

actually suffered. Yet days of really bitter cold are the exception, not the rule ; and by keeping the stoves crammed with wood, the living-rooms are commonly comfortable, even on such days. To be sure, there will be a chilliness apparent along the walls and in the corners; and in really keen weather it is impossible to keep a room warm on the windy side of the house. The north-west gales will blow through anything. In large houses, with the stove rooms on the south side, keeping warm is less difficult. Prob-ably much of the time a country sit-ting-room is too warm, rather than too cold. The inhab-itants feel obliged to have a contrast with the frost outside, and in many farmhouses the air in the little sitting-room is kept fairly baked. The inmates would think themselves seriously chilly in a coal-fire temperature of sev-enty degrees.

Sawing Ice

A wood fire in a sheet-iron stove sends out a truly blistering heat if it is attended to; but if continuous attention is not given, it fluctuates. It may amount to about the same as being cooked in an oven one half-hour; and inside of the next half-hour the fire goes down till the cold creeps in at the cracks, and you begin to shiver. That reminds you to put some wood in the stove, and set the cooking process in opera-tion again.

The New England winter is felt most in those households where the stock of sawed wood is allowed to run low, and the " women folks " are obliged to resort to constant appeal to the men to get enough to keep the fires going, or are compelled to saw it themselves. Take a real country town right through, and there are a good many farmers who do not keep up their wood supply as they should, and some of them are short of wood the year around. This state of affairs is called by the more forehanded neighbors " shiftlessness." Sometimes there is not only a lack of sawed wood, but the whole woodpile is allowed to get depleted almost to the last stick. The farmer is then obliged to resort to the woods for a new supply ; and the housewife has to burn green wood, which is her especial detestation. She can only make the best of it ; and that best is to always keep a supply of green sticks under the stove or in the oven drying, while they await their turn to become a part of the fire. The drying wood gives the room a peculiar and not unpleasant odor.

Winter work is not so arduous or long continued as that of other seasons of the year. Aside from the regular work of looking after the stock and odd jobs of tinkering and tool-mending about his premises, the farmer's chief concern is his woodpile. If he has a good deal of woodland, chopping and logging form an important feature of the winter. If he has little, he often hires himself out to those who want help in the woods.

The best parts of the trees which make good timber are hauled away as logs to the sawmills, and anything that will serve for railroad ties or telegraph poles is likewise reserved. Trees that have no timber value, and the tops of those that have, are cut into four-foot lengths, split if necessary, and piled up ready to be sledded off. It is the method, usually, to cut the particular patch of forest selected for work clear of all standing wood that has any value for sawmill or burning purposes. Spring finds the land bare, save for the brush-heaps, a few saplings, and an occasional gaunt and decayed old trunk still upright. The mountain sides and the rocky hills and hollows are the chief homes

WINTER WORK ON THE POND

of the forests; but the willows and poplars along the river-banks
are sometimes a source of woodpile supply.

In some towns are shops where tobacco-sorting or broom-tying
has a place among winter industries.   Such shops are famous

FISHING THROUGH THE ICE

lounging-places; and the affairs of the town, State, and nation, and
in particular those of the neighbors, are settled there daily.   The
loungers and workers have among them often very clever mimics,
who can take off anybody and anything; and for picturesqueness
and quaint Yankee humor their talk at best is unequalled.

Where there is proximity to ponds or large streams, the farmers have little ice-houses back of their homes which must be filled.
Some morning the oxen, or the horses, are hitched to the long
sled; and with saws, poles, and grappling-irons, the men-folks start
for the ice.   It is sloppy work; but there are chances of diversify-

ing it by taking along fishing-tackle, and establishing a skirmish-line of fish-holes in the neighborhood.

Winter is a time of increased social activity. There are more "doings" at the church ; the singing-school starts the first week of December at the Town Hall ; and the Chautauqua Club gathers in turn at the members' houses every Friday evening. Perhaps the villagers start a lyceum at the schoolhouse, and speak pieces, sing songs, have dialogues, and debate, "Which is the most important animal, the cat or the dog?" and other important questions. The chief object of the lyceums is the having a lot of fun ; and what is sought in debate is not culture, or display of one's powers as an orator, or the solution of great questions, but amuse-

BREAKING OUT THE ROAD

ment. Culture, oratory, etc., come in incidentally; but the serious old-time lyceum, which discussed regularly great national and moral questions, is not to be found in many regions to-day. But the cat-

and-dog debate, or the discussion of such topics as "Which is the most destructive element, fire or water?" and "Which does it cost the most to dress, a man or a woman?" are not without their virtues; for they at least stir thought and furnish health-ful amusement.

For the children there are sliding and skating; and some youth, about this time, suggests the wild scheme of clubbing together and hiring an omnibus for a grand sleighride of all the young people. Some fine evening they all pile into the long-sleigh, and drive off behind the four horses with their jingling bells, for ten or twelve miles, and have a turkey supper at midnight at a tavern. Afterward they may have a dance. Not always, for dancing is considered a doubtful amusement by many country families; and, indeed, in the country dances the company is not always a choice one, nor the hours seasonable, and if the older members of the family object to having their sons and daughters concerned in them, they are not altogether without good reason for so objecting.

One winter task is that of breaking out the roads after the heavy storms. In the lowlands this is only an occasional neces-sity. But among the hills nearly every storm blocks the roads. Thaws in the uplands are infrequent; and snow piles on snow, and a drift forms in the lee of every stone wall and hummock. Many roads, or parts of them, are entirely abandoned; and a "winter road" is made through the woods or across the open fields. Even a light snow, if it is dry and accompanied by wind, will fill the exposed roads, and heap up the drifts with astonishing rapidity.

The breaking-out process is accomplished by hitching a pair of horses to the front bob of a sled, at one side of which is fas-tened a plough. Two men are needed to engineer the contri-vance, — one as driver, one as plough-holder. When a drift is encountered through which the team cannot struggle, the men resort to shovelling. It is a rough-hewed track that the plough leaves behind, and, until travel has smoothed it, not a very comfortable one to travel over.

Among the hills, only the high schools hold winter sessions.

TURNING OUT THROUGH THE FIELDS

The scholars of the primary schools live so far away, as a rule, that it would be a real hardship for them to attempt to get to school regularly through the snows. The big boys, who a generation or two ago used to come in every winter to the little district schoolhouses, now have a high school open to them. It is very apparent that these boys are the sons of their fathers, for they worry the high-school teachers very much as their ancestors used to worry the teachers of the district schools. Display of smartness and insubordination is still altogether too common in New England schools.

Aside from the hilly and mountainous regions, the country schools all have their regular winter term, that begins the first week in December. Soon after eight o'clock each school-day morning the children tie up their ears, put on their cloaks and mittens and overshoes, and, with their sleds dragging behind, go stubbing along through the snow toward the schoolhouse. Those

THE HORSE-SHEDS ON SUNDAY

who come from more than half a mile have in hand their tin dinner-pails ; and, on stormy days, even the child that lives just across the road feels abused if it cannot carry its dinner.

The more advanced children of the outlying districts of a town

have a long ride before them each winter morning to the academy
at the Centre, a distance of perhaps three or four miles. They
go in all kinds of weather. Neither storm nor cold can keep them
at home. It sends a sympathetic shiver through one to look out
and see them drive past in the gray frostiness of the early morning. The case seems plainly one of getting education under diffi-
culties. But they know how to bundle up ; and if there is hardship,
they seem not to realize it. Perhaps they are even to be envied.
The experience gives them hardiness ; and the long drives back
and forth, with whatever they contain of storms and cold and mis-
haps, will in after life be among the most pleasantly treasured
memories.

Church-going is not much affected by the winter weather. A
storm will keep a certain number at home, whatever the season.
But, if the roads are passable, the man who is in the habit of going
to church continues to go the year round, independent of heat or
cold. On a crisp day of sunshine and good sleighing, the ride to
church, accompanied by the cheerful music of a string of bells, is
a real pleasure.

On the whole, the New England winter is by no means dubious, and its people find it enjoyable. If there is some suffering
or discomfort, it is doubtless far less than in the cities ; and it may
as well be recognized that Utopia has been dreamed of, never yet
realized.

II

A WINTER RIDE

BUSINESS called me one winter from my home in the Connecticut valley to the hill country in the extreme western part of Massachusetts. I could go by train; but it seemed to me it would make a pleasant and interesting ride, and I concluded to drive instead. It was March first. The night before there had been a slight snowstorm, that ended in a dash of sleet and rain. The rain had crusted the snow; and, in spite of the brisk wind that blew, the snow did not drift. There was a change, however, as soon as I began to ascend the hills beyond the lowlands. It was only in the valley that it had rained, and in the upland opens the wind whisked the sifting snow across the fields in a way to make one shiver. The air was keen and chilling, but by getting out and walking I could always get into a glow in a short time. The road was a long uphill way, mostly through the wood, where the wind roared continually in the crashing tree-tops. The woods seemed very lifeless; though I sometimes saw a rabbit-track, or heard a squirrel's squeak, or saw a lonely crow flapping hungrily through the wind. Once I heard a chopper's axe not far away among the trees, but I could not see the man.

When, at long intervals, I met a team, I had to manœuvre to turn out so that I would dodge drifts and deep places. If the team I met was loaded, I was expected to give it the whole road. My horse would flounder out into the untrodden snow ,at the side of the double trail of the roadway, and stand there buried clear up to his body till the team passed. Then we struggled back into the road and went on. The roads had been ploughed out, and the snow was piled up in high ridges on each side.

At noon I stopped to give the horse a feed, and eat a lunch I had with me. A little later, when we were again on the way, I met a wood-team; and a short distance farther on I saw a place in the woods where the team had burrowed out two or three woodpiles. Beyond that no team had left a track that day. I now approached a bare hill-top. The road was worse drifted than it had been before, and the snow was whirling across in clouds.

The prospect was dubious, but I did not like to turn back. I got out, and led the horse. The horse sank in more than I did, and the sleigh cut in so that the snow heaped up against the dashboard. Then, of a sudden, the horse stepped out of the track, and nearly disappeared from sight. At the same time he seemed to get his legs tangled up, so that he could barely move. I thought it was time to stop; and I trod around the horse a little, unhitched him, and induced him to flounder on to a less drifted spot, where he stood, whitened with snow, with the harness draggling about him, while I considered what I should do next. Far over the hill one or two farmhouses were in sight. If I could get over the stone wall to the left, I might make my way across the fields and get help. But it seemed best I should try to help myself first. It was hopeless going ahead; and with great pains I lifted the sleigh about, worked it along to a shallower spot, got my horse back between the thills,

and then plunged along out of the drifts to where, in the shelter
of the woods, the roadway was clear.

I had not given up my journey, but simply went back till
I could find some other road over the hills.   Not till I had
gone six or eight miles did I find such a road.   Then began
another long ascent through the woods, that brought me, just

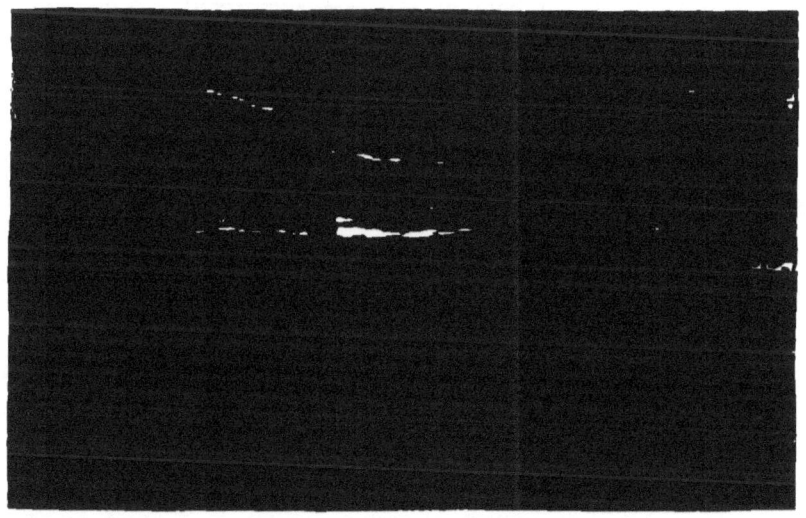

A HILLTOP VILLAGE

after sundown, in sight of the outlying houses of Littletown
village on an open hill-top close ahead.   As soon as the road
left the woods it was buried in great drifts, with a deep trench
dug through them for a thoroughfare.   Snow had blown in and
narrowed the trench; but it still seemed possible to make the
passage, and, I went on.   Soon I thought it safer to get out
and walk.   The horse was bound to keep in the lowest part of
the trench; and, in spite of all I could do, the sleigh was slid
up on the snowbank, and my effects were pitched out into the

drifts. I stopped the horse, righted the sleigh somewhat, got my things aboard, and tried again. Within a rod, over went the sleigh a second time; and matters were worse than ever, for I could not get the sleigh right side up till I had unhitched the horse. I hastened to get back into it some of my valuables that were being covered by the sifting snows, and then went forward to reconnoitre. From far up the road a man was approaching with a staff and a bundle. He was not exactly a ministering angel; but he served just as well, for he readily consented to help me pull the sleigh up through the worst of the near drifts. When we had done that, I suggested leaving it there over night; but the man said it would be buried out of sight by morning. So we hitched in the horse, and the man went ahead to tread a path for him, while I followed, leading him; and we staggered along till he said he guessed I could go alone the rest of the way — I'd find a hotel a half a mile farther. He said his home was off on a side road, so drifted no team could get to it.

The horse and I, in time, came to a house which had a drift in the yard that nearly buried the L out of sight. A boy and a man who had been watching my approach from a stable-door came out to interview me, and said they would go along, and show me the way to the hotel. In their company I crossed the road, went through the dooryard of a house opposite, back of the barn, under the apple-trees, and picked an uncertain way across the fields. In the end, under the light of a full moon whose round, surprised face was looking out of the east, I reached the hotel. This hotel was a big, verandaed barn of a building, which in warm weather was the resort of many summer boarders, but in winter was well-nigh deserted.

Supper was spread for me in a little corner sitting-room, where were the selectmen and town-clerk of the community, waiting to register voters in anticipation of the March town-meeting. They said every voter in town was registered but one, and they didn't believe he'd come. Still, it was the law they should be there that night, and there they were. Chief among these officials was the tall, bony chairman of selectmen, a politician of some note in the region, and the leading man of the church and town. He talked in the vernacular, with the usual Yankee twang, as did all the others. A youngish man named Harris kept the hotel. His assistants were a red-headed and capable young woman who presided in the kitchen, and a young man who had at one time been a reporter on the *New York Sun*, but

SHARPENING HIS AXE

now had plans to make his fortune by running a maple-sugar camp in the spring.

The big coal-stove kept the room comfortably warm, I thought ;

but the town-officials, in spite of their staying all through the long evening, did not take their extra wraps off, not even the chairman of the selectmen, who had on two overcoats.

The men did not think much of these upland winters. One said, "I told my wife that if I had any amount of sense I wouldn't spend the winter on Littletown hill. It's a leetle too tough."

They had a Chautauqua club in town with fifteen members, that met every week at the members' houses. Some of the attendants live far out of the centre, and they could not get together much before eight or half-past. Two hours are spent in the regular exercises; and then, if there is time afterwards, they have games, but it is usually too late.

Not more than one-fourth of the three hundred inhabitants go to church. There is little opposition to religion — the non-church-goers are simply indifferent. A few of the farmers, when they happen to feel like it, work on Sundays just as on a week-day. The preacher who for many years had presided over the Littletown flock had recently, at the age of eighty-one, received a call to a neighboring town, and had left them. They had a church fund that brought in two hundred and fifty dollars a year, and they usually intended to pay the minister a salary of five hundred dollars. In addition he was given the use of the parsonage and the fifteen-acre farm that goes with it. While without a minister the two deacons preside in the pulpit. They alternate with each other in reading sermons on Sunday mornings, and take turns in reading hymns and making prayers. Sunday evenings, and again on Thursday evenings, when the weather permits, they have a prayer-meeting; but, just as in most country places, this attracts few attendants. Every other week the Ladies' Aid Society give a sociable at one of the homes; and, besides the refreshments served, they have humorous recitations, music, etc., not to mention the collection which is taken up.

Toward ten o'clock the town-fathers buttoned up their coats
and departed; and then the landlord, at my request, guided me
up-stairs to bed. In my room a fire was burning smokily in
a rusty little stove. It seemed inclined to go out altogether;
but about midnight it burst into cheerful flaming, and through
the cracks and open damper cast flickering patches of light out
on the walls and ceiling. The wind blew furiously and gustily
all through the night. It shook the house, teetered the bed-
stead, and kept my window curtain scraping on the casing till
I crawled out and attempted to run it up. It wouldn't run; and
I had to tie its tassel to a chair, and swing it out into the room.

Next morning when I looked out of my window at half-past
seven, the sun was shining brightly, and it continued to shine
all day. Just as I finished breakfast the stage arrived from the
town beyond. This stage passes over the hill in the early morning every week-day, on its way to the county town, and returns
in the middle of the afternoon. It is drawn by two horses. In
the winter the vehicle is a rusty, two-seated sleigh; in the summer a rusty, three-seated, square top-carriage. The driver came
stamping into the hotel in his big fur coat, with the leather mail-
bag. Two or three shovellers accompanied him. He doubted
whether he had better attempt to go farther. His only freight
was the mail-bag and a single passenger. The shovellers went
out, and in a whirlwind of snow attacked one of the drifts. The
task looked hopeless, and the driver offered a shoveller two dollars
to take the mail-bag down on foot. He accepted, and tramped
away in company with the single passenger. The rest of us
hurried in-doors, and the driver said he would spend the day
playing " pitch." The ex-reporter and he got out their card-
packs, their cigars and cigarettes, called for a pitcher of cider,
and sat down with a stand between them in the corner to play.
The landlord looked on; and so did one of the shovellers, an old
man named Dagon. The latter was a leading Adventist and

Spiritualist of the region, a religious man and an earnest exhorter, and capable expounder of his views when occasion offered. Yet he was a man to whom a drop of liquor did not come amiss now and then, and the players asked him companionably if he had any spirits over at his house.

"No," he said; "I wish I had."

SAWING WOOD

The stage-driver had no liquor, and neither had the ex-reporter ; so they all said it was a dry time, and turned for comfort to the cider-pitcher.

There were quite a number of "Advents" in the town ; and they owned a little chapel, but held no regular meetings. Some of them attended the Congregational church. Several years before, there had been an Advent revival, which threw the believers into great excitement. They neglected their work, they expected the world to come to an end so soon, and thought they must be watching, and converting others. Thus some, who were formerly well-to-do, were now quite poor. They still kept up their organization, and when they had a meeting would make fervent appeals to the brethren to hold out to the end. To be sure there were only a few of the faithful, but did not the Bible say that at the Lord's coming there would be but a few? Mr. Dagon said that it was prophesied in the Scriptures that the moon should be darkened, the stars fall, and Christ would appear to gather his chosen. In 1789 came the fulfilment of the first part of the prophecy, for then the sun was darkened. In 1833 the stars fell; and now we only await the final sign. He thought it would come soon, but he did not know just how soon. The Advent belief, he said, was that the dead sleep till Christ's coming, — all except two, Enoch and Elijah, who at once entered into glory. They do not believe in hell, but that the wicked and those who do not accept Christ will be as ashes trodden under foot, annihilated, just as much as any one can be annihilated. There will be a new heaven and a new earth, and Christ will come here to reign over his followers.

A man came in after a time, and wanted to borrow a file. He was a rusty-looking fellow, good-natured, they said, — good worker for other people, but too easy and too slack a manager to do well for himself. Mr. Dagon asked him if he played.

"I don't play for money," he replied, "only for cigars and whiskey or cider."

So he and the old gentleman sat down and played a game of high-low-jack. Two or three other people happened in, and loitered about the stove. To the question, "Had the wind gone down?" the answer was always, "Yes, gone down over the hill toward Millburg."

"It blows the stuffin' right out o' me," remarked one. "How'd your thermometer stand here this mornin'?" he continued.

" Two b'low," responded the landlord.

"Well, you've got a pretty accommodatin' thermometer, I reckon. 'Twas ten b'low down to our place."

Late in the morning we saw from the window a pair of horses struggling through the drifts, and floundering so deeply it seemed as if they were in danger of being altogether buried. The driver urged them on till at length they came through to the hotel. He had come up from Millburg to collect butter, eggs, etc., and had broken down in the drifts, and left his sleigh behind. He stayed thawing out till noon, when he fed his horses, ate his dinner from a tin pail, and then we saw his blue frock-coat moving off down the road through the whirling snows.

Dinner was served in a big chilly kitchen, where was a cooking-stove and a great cluttering of dishes and odds and ends. After we had eaten, we again adjourned to the little corner-room where the big stove was. The landlord pulled the dog off the lounge, and lay down there himself, and most of the company had a smoke.

Our window looked out on a wide sweep of white fields, misted by scurrying drift ; and far off were lines of half-wooded hills. Late in the afternoon the shoveller arrived with the mail-bag. Then the stage-driver got into his big fur coat, and the eight men of us who happened to be at the hotel went out and dragged his sleigh through the wild snowblasts over the drifts of the near road-way, while he followed after with the horses. On we went with the sleigh across lots, over stone walls and through dooryards, now and then dodging along the roadway for a piece, till we came to a turn where the highway left the hill-top. Then six of us returned, and left the driver and the other two to make their way as best they could.

I continued on beyond the hotel as far as the woods where I had first encountered the hill-top drifts the night before. In some places the way was blown bare, down to the dirt ; in others, the snow was heaped in masses little short of mountainous. Every

AFTER A STORM

house had one or two big windrows in its lee.   In the final drift
at the edge of the woods was a heavy two-horse sled high up on
the snow, yet nearly buried.   On it were blankets and a broken
bridle.   The neck-yoke was stuck in the snow a bit ahead, and
farther along was more broken harness.   The spot where I had
thought of leaving my sleigh was covered many feet deep with
hard-packed snow.

By the time I turned back it was getting dusky, and the round
red moon had come up in the blue-gray haze over the eastern
snow hills, and looked across the frozen landscape and into the
ruddy glow of the west, where the sun had just set.   It was no
joking matter facing the fierce wind and the biting particles of
flying ice, and I was glad to get back to the hotel.

On the morning following the sky was grayed with gathering
clouds.   The distant valley was veiled with a light haze.   The
wind had died down, and it was possible to move about with some
comfort ; and by eight o'clock all the able-bodied men in town
were out with shovels and teams clearing the roads.   The shovellers charge the town fifteen cents an hour, and "find themselves."
That does not infer that they get lost, but means they must furnish their own board and lodging.

Soon teams began to appear on their way to market, and went
dodging through the fields and bumping over the stone-walls.   In
reply to my remark that they didn't often get drifts higher than
that, did they ? the inhabitants would say, " Wal, I do' know —
we sometimes get some of 'em a little higher, but not every
winter."

At the parsonage a small apple-tree was buried up to its top
twigs.   The shovellers commented on this apple-tree to the effect
that now was a "good time for the minister to pick his apples —
wouldn't have to use no ladder."

I asked if it was going to storm.   One said, after looking at
the sky, that it would snow within twenty-four hours.   But the

blacksmith was sure the next storm would be rain ; " For," said he, " I heard the crows cawin' round the fields like blazes yesterday."

Down at the edge of the woods were a dozen men shovelling in the big drift there. They had a rough trench through, when along came a heavy two-horse sled with a ton of butter on board. Into the trench went the team, and down went the horses almost out of sight, and the thing came to a stop. Then there was shouting, and tugging at the sled, and shovelling; and again and again the team started forward, only to come to a halt within a yard or two, with the horses as much entangled in the snow as if their legs were tied. But perseverance brought them through at last ; and the men went back to dig their trench deeper.

GETTING A TEAM THROUGH THE DRIFT

The sky, as the morning waned, continued to darken ; and presently the first flakes of a storm came whirling out of the west. The shovellers said there was not much use trying to journey over those hills in such drifts, unless I was obliged to ; and by the time I got ready to come back there would like enough be a thaw, and then the slumping would make the going worse still. The result was that, when I returned to the hotel, I got my team, and turned back toward home. It was laborious travelling ; but I got along very well till I entered the trench in the great drift near the woods. In the midst of that I sighted a team coming up the hollow toward me. My landlord with his shovel had come along to see me well started on the homeward way ; and he shouted at the other driver, and hurled swear-words at him, till he woke up, and came to a stop. The team we met was a double one, and had on a load. It was our duty, therefore, to make way. We selected a shallow place, dug some, unhitched the horse, swung the sleigh out, got the horse into the drift, and let the other team pass. Then we fixed up, and I went on alone. I reached home without further mishap, and the next week made the journey I had planned by railroad.

III

TOWN–MEETING

IN most of our New England towns the day set apart for town-meeting is the first Monday in March. Winter has begun to lose its keenness by that time, and the unsettled days that prelude spring have arrived. With the coming of March, spells of weather are to be expected when the sun's rays are full of heat, and the snow softens into slush; and brown earth patches on the hillsides and muddy streaks in the roadways appear with astonishing quickness. But, as a rule, on town-meeting day there is still sleighing, and not infrequently the cold is sharp and blustering.

The meeting begins at nine o'clock in the morning, and continues till such a time in the afternoon as all business is finished. Only a handful of people, aside from the town-officers, are present at nine o'clock. Most of the farmers have not yet finished their morning's work; and, besides, they do not expect anything of special interest or importance will be done before ten or half-past. The first thing is to ballot for a moderator. Usually the friends of some particular man who wants the honor have arranged previously that this man shall have the

office; and they are on nand, and promptly elect their man.
The person elected is usually a man of some vigor, with considerable self-confidence and power of voice. After he takes
the chair the town-clerk reads the articles of the town-warrant,
and the village minister offers a short prayer.

In what follows I describe the town-meeting as I know it
in one of the older valley farming-towns; but in most particulars
the story would be much the same in any New England country
place. The town-hall is a low white building, with a pillared
front, that stands next the church. The church horse-sheds are

AT THE TOWN HALL.

full of teams by the middle of the forenoon. Other teams have
been left at the hotel and at the near neighbors.' There are

not many stay-at-homes — nearly all the men-folks of the town
are out. But the large majority of them are present, not because of a serious interest in town affairs, but for a holiday —
for the fun they can get out of it. These people like to vote,
and they have a personal interest in the license question and
in the choice of a few of the town-officers. But it is extremely
rare that one of them says anything publicly in the meeting.
Privately they carry on long conversations, and they only listen
when the speaking gets exciting or funny. They like to loiter
on the porch outside, and at the back of the room. The moderator has at intervals to ask them to keep quiet, or he requests
the constable to keep the door shut and to preserve order. But
the constable is a stout little man, whose eyes twinkle, and who
seems to take disorder as a joke rather than seriously. He trans-
fers the dignity of his presence to the neighborhood of the dis-
orderly, and winks, and makes a mild suggestion or two, and shuts
the door; and the voices of the social voters in the back of the
room, which had grown loud, resume their former undertone.

The crowd that gathers on town-meeting day is an uncom-
monly interesting one. They come from the highways and the
byways. They are not the same people one sees at church.
Even the church-going have not their Sunday appearances. Once
in a while there is a man who has on his best clothes, but he is
the exception. The majority are in their every-day working
clothes, and they keep their hats on; and hardly anyone takes his
overcoat off, no matter how hot it gets. As a whole, the crowd
looks coarse and unkempt. They repel rather than attract. One
does not feel he would like to live in the same house with most of
them. The way they slouch around, and the promiscuous way
they have of spitting their tobacco juice about, both indoors and
out, does not speak very well for either their cleanliness or for
their mental calibre. Neither is a well-rounded health characteristic of the men one sees. There is a certain toughness that

comes from a life out-of-doors, but not a natural, well-balanced virility. The young men are some of a blowsy redness, some thin-blooded and pallid; the old men are withered or gnarled. It is plain that many, particularly those that represent the foreign ele-

A FERRY MAN

ment, are drinkers. The majority of country people have not such habits as make for their best health. But, as far as that goes, neither have the majority such habits anywhere.

The hall interior is a big square room, with tall windows along the sides. It has the somewhat battered rustiness characteristic of such public places. There are two stoves in opposite corners of the room, with long reaches of stove-pipe crawling along the wall, high up to the chimney, in a third corner. The centre of the room is occupied by several lines of green settees. Up in front is a long platform; and on it, behind a long table, sit the

three selectmen and the moderator. At a desk a little to one side
is the town-clerk. It seems to depend on half a dozen men to do
most of the necessary, as well as the unnecessary, talking of the
day ; and these are the men who see that the routine business is
pushed along and done in order. They sit scattered about somewhere near the front of the hall.

Now and then one of these men will get up, and go over to
another to give him a hint or have a consultation. They visit the
selectmen's table often, to keep posted, and to make and take sug-
gestions. Sometimes several of them will gather for an earnest
talk with the officials about the town-clerk's desk ; and all business,
as far as the rest of the assembly is concerned, is at a standstill.
The moderator fingers his mallet and smiles helplessly, and the
lone selectman whose duty it is to turn the crank of the ballot-
machine that registers the votes on license is the only one to keep
his place. He looks at the audience as if he acknowledged that
this was not business-like, but what could he do about it ?

When a question is put, these half-dozen men who seem naturally to be the chief actors of the day, and a few others, are the
only ones usually to say " Aye " or " No." The rest of the crowd
simply looks on. They do not voice their opinions, either in votes
or in their remarks, except in the continuous rumble of their conversation.

When there is balloting to be done, several wooden boxes are
put on the table where the selectmen sit. These boxes have
mostly been made for the purpose, and are painted red, and have a
label pasted on the side to show what office the box receives votes
for. When there are not enough of the regular boxes, some old
soap-box from the neighboring store serves instead. The voters
file in front of the selectmen's table, back of a little fence, their
names are called off by the moderator, the selectmen check them
on the voting-list, they deposit their ballots, and pass on. Nearly
all the men take off their hats when they pass the voting-boxes,

but once in a while some old fellow will not observe this ceremony.   The ballots are usually printed slips ; the candidates look
out for that, and have them placed in the hands of their friends
for distribution.   Often there is only one candidate for an office,
a man who has served as town-clerk, or whatever the office is, for
many years.   He receives every vote cast.   When it is plain that
things are going without opposition, a motion is frequently made
in the midst of the voting to turn the box down to save time.
For some minor office there is occasionally such slight interest
that only one vote is cast.

Considerable joking is intermixed with the work of the day.
There is real wit in some of the remarks.   The voters always enjoy the nominating and electing of fence-viewers, measurers of
wood and bark, and field-drivers.   The two former offices were
perhaps very useful fifty or a hundred years ago, but they entail
slight duties in these days.   Yet a man has to be elected for each
district, and the name is presented that seems to be funniest
in that connection.   Neither have the field-drivers much to do,
but such caring for stray animals as is necessary is not regarded
as a job to " hanker " for.   Some man of the district who has
married within the past year, or some young fellow who the fall
before cast his first vote, is usually selected for the office.

A good deal of respect is felt and shown for the town-meeting
routine.   The educational influence of the meeting is undoubtedly
good.   It is a legislature on a small scale, a miniature House of
Commons.   The speaking is mostly pithy and direct, and easily
drops into humor.   There are the droning men, but they make
themselves heard only occasionally ; and some men of ability are
too long-winded, and repeat themselves tiresomely, and there are
those who indulge in spread-eagleism.   The latter is particularly
ineffective.   A few short, sharp sentences are the rule.   Slips in
grammar are not infrequent, even from the town-fathers ; and
while the nasal New England drawl that makes " down " " daown "

is not always prominent, it is never altogether absent in the speeches of the day.

Every town has its cliques. There are certain men the cliques want elected, certain measures they want carried. In some towns and in some years they do not make themselves very much felt, but again they occasion very sharp fighting. There are towns so composed that there are two parties with opposing interests; for instance, where there is a farm region and a manufacturing village in the same township, or two farm villages of about the same size. Whichever gets the upper hand neglects the other part, and appropriates and spends money for its own particular advantage.

THE FERRY LANDING

There is no lack of excitement on town-meeting day in such places; and some of the more excitable men will shake fists and call names, and make it necessary for their friends to restrain them by laying hold of their coat-tails. This sort of thing awakens intense enthusiasm on the part of the audience at the back of the room.

A town is very apt to have one or two chronic objectors or cranks in it. They make business lag, but they usually amuse the crowd. There are old-fashioned men, with queerly trimmed beards, and long hair combed down in front of their ears after the style of fifty years ago, who denounce change, and think the town should pattern after the ways and economics of the time when they were young. They especially despise any new-fangled notions about schools, and think boarding around for the teachers, and plenty of licking for the scholars, and a continuation of all children in the district schools until they are prepared for the academy, is the best system of education ever devised. That was the way they were educated, and it is very clear to them that those old schools turned out better specimens than the present schools do.

But in all places where partianship has not run mad, the voters at the close of a discussion will adopt the view that has been made to appear most sensible. They want to do the fair thing. The chairman of the selectmen is the person who does more talking usually than any other citizen. He has to explain recommendations made, and defend the expenditures and decisions of the board for the past year, whenever these are questioned. The chairman of selectmen in the town I speak of has a salary of one hundred dollars. It seems as if the work and talk of the town-meeting day alone were worth nearly that. What he says is almost always reasonable ; and the voters feel that he is, as he says, " working for the best interests of the town," and they give him their support.

In towns where the saloon and anti-saloon elements are at all evenly divided, there is an immense underground activity of the drinkers. They are sure to be on hand, all of them, and to act

A FIRE ON THE EDGE OF THE WOODS

as one man. If a town has a poor-house and a drinking-place, I think these voters care little what else it lacks. The man who runs the hotel is around during the morning at the polls, to see how things look ; but later he has to attend to business. He serves free drinks that day to the faithful, and the faithful are thirsty and call often. When, in the middle of the afternoon, it is announced by the moderator that license has carried the day, the visages of the drinkers light up joyfully ; and they shout, and stamp the floor, and clap hands. Then there is a sudden quiet. Every soul of them has deserted the hall and public business, and gone down to the hotel to celebrate in the flowing bowl the sweet delights of victory.

Some of the humorous sparring of the day comes on such questions as the following : One man, named Bates, thinks the best way to collect taxes is to allow a five-per-cent discount for prompt-

OLD FRIENDS

ness. Another man says there is no gain in that, even for the man that takes the discount. " Now," he says, "a man like Mr. Bates, with plenty of ready money, pays his tax and gets his discount. But the man who doesn't have ready money just waits till he's made up that amount of interest before he pays. So it amounts to the same thing in the end." There was just enough truth in this statement of the case to make it funny.

The selectmen proposed that the town should buy a roller. The choice lay between three styles, that cost respectively $185, $200, and $225. The selectmen thought the one for $185 hardly suitable, and a motion was made to appropriate $200. This was objected to, because it seemed possible it was wisest to get the $225 one. The man who made the motion then got up and said he expected that with a $200 appropriation they would get the $225 machine. If the manufacturers knew that was all the town had to pay they would, " in these hard times," let it go for that. The selectmen could beat them down if they wanted to, easy. But it wasn't clear that this was practical, and even on the $200 machine there was freight to pay. So another man got up and explained it was not wise to make any hard limits in the appropriation, and moved an amendment to the motion that would make it read $200, or *thereabouts*. But the voters took the view that there was too much freedom in that word, and they made the limit $200. No doubt they were right in thinking that at least the $200 machine could be had, freight paid.

An old covered wooden bridge in town was badly in need of repairs. A man got up and said he would like to know what the matter with it was. He'd never heard a word but that the bridge was all right. At once a quick-witted, but illiterate, Irishman jumped up, and said, " Mr. Moderator, it's kind o' springy, and it makes a man dizzy to cross it."

This bridge was on the road to a large town, where many of the farmers sold produce. This large town was a famous place for liquor-selling. As soon as the Irishman dropped into his seat, another man said he guessed they didn't find the bridge springy going down, but it was when they were coming back, after they'd taken something in the town. Up popped the Irishman. " Yes," he said, "that is so — the bridge does not shake when we are going to the town. That is because the wagon has a heavy load on that keeps it down. But when we come back we have no load, and then it is springy."

A slick young man from a city bridge company was present ; and he was given a chance to address the meeting, and say what sort of a bridge was best for the place. An iron bridge of the sort needed would cost something under one thousand dollars. " Well," was the comment, "if one thousand dollars is your outside price, what is your inside price ? "

The young man did not quite like this question, and he hesitated. " Will you build it for five hundred dollars ? " asked the man.

" No," said the bridge-builder.

" Will you build it for six hundred, then ? " was the question. " A thousand dollars would repair the old one, and I thought five hundred ought to be enough to build a new one."

At noon the company adjourned for dinner. Some went home, some went to their friends ; but a large number stepped over to the church, where the ladies of the parish were ready with oysters, coffee, and accessories at twenty-five cents a person. The sixteen or eighteen dollars they took in would do for some necessary parish work, of which there is never a time when there is lack.

The clatter and the chatter of the vestry at eating-time are very enlivening ; but there is not much time to spare after eating is over, and the horses in the sheds have been fed. Still, one has time for a cigar ; and, as treating is the order of the day, the cigars pass about freely, and staid middle-aged men, whom you will hardly see with a cigar at any other time in the year, will be smoking one town-meeting day. At the post-office, the selectmen have invested in several boxes of cigars, not too expensive an article, and everybody is at liberty to help himself. The selectmen, of course, have hundred-dollar positions at stake, and they want to keep all the voters good-natured toward them. The odor of tobacco was apparent in the hall in the morning; but in the afternoon the cigar-smoking in the rear of the hall is constant, the air turns hazy, and the atmosphere, to the unaccustomed, is sickening. It is enough to make a woman-suffragist of a non-smoker, however violently he might be opposed to the general principle. Men will not respect signs or public places; yet, to their credit, it can still be said that they respect the presence of a woman.

Toward dusk the last article in the warrant has been talked over and voted on, and the meeting adjourns. Every one then hurries off home to get the farm-work done before supper. The women-folks say they would know where the men had been, if only by the odor of their clothes. Indeed, that tobacco odor is so ingrained that it takes some days for it to wear entirely away.

IV

HOW SPRING COMES

THE poet pictures spring as a beautiful maiden coming down a woodland path. Her face is wreathed in smiles, and her arms are full of flowers. Then, too, when you turn the pages of an art catalogue, and find a painting entitled "Spring," you may be pretty sure the original will be some hillside where the apple-trees put forth their clouds of pink-and-white blossoms, or a bit beside some stream or pond where the green mists of the fresh starting leafage are mirrored in the quiet waters.

This is spring idealized. It is true, yet it is not the whole truth. With the coming of March the New England native begins to look for a thaw, which, unlike the other thaws of the winter, shall be a finality. The other thaws, as, for instance, "the January thaw," which the oldest inhabitant always expects with no small degree of confidence, only temporize with winter. A cold snap of redoubled severity always lurks in their wake. When the March thaw comes, however, the farmer has a feeling that spring is not far off. He finds a harbinger of approaching mildness in the way the crows caw, in the woodpecker's signalling as he hammers away at a dead limb on the maple-tree before the

house, in the south winds that blow; and when, at length, he
sights a bluebird, that settles it — spring is really coming.

Yet there is still a sharp frost nearly every night. Even
before the sun has set you can feel the chill of the approaching
night; and the mud stiffens, and splinters of ice begin to form on
the roadway puddles. Winter is loath to acknowledge himself
conquered, and he frequently sweeps down and does battle with
the gentler forces of the South long after these have begun to
assert themselves. Sometimes he comes with a whirl of snow
that whitens all the fields, and gives the landscape a midwinter

SPRING AMONG THE NEW ENGLAND HILLS

look again. But even if it is a blizzard that buries the country,
and drifts the roadway, the snow lies lightly, and it settles and
disappears very quickly.

Again, winter comes with wild blasts of wind that make every wooden house at all exposed vibrate and totter, and set every loose blind, door, and window about the place to rattling and banging. It whistles about the eaves and chimney-tops, and makes strange creakings and buzzings among the crevices and loose boards of the barn. It turns the roads to flint, and petrifies in them every rut and roughness. At such times Mr. Farmer gets well shaken up, even when he travels in his "spring wagon," — a vehicle which has nothing to do with the season, but so named because it has springs to cushion its movements.

Snowstorms sometimes come as late as the middle of April. The late snowstorms usually occur in the night; and it is always with something of surprise that one awakes in the morning, and looks out to find yesterday's brown earth transformed to a world of white. The snow is apt to be soft and clinging; and all the trees and fences bear feathery loads that give every view, whether of field or village street, a magic charm, and make the aisles of the woods fairy-land. These late storms are known as "sugar-snows," and are supposed to make the maple sap flow more freely —why, I do not know. A day's sunlight will usually dispel them, and leave only shreds behind where some chance shadow gave protection.

To a degree this kind of snow is also deemed a beneficence, in that it is said to take the frost out of the ground, and "settle the going." But its first effect on the going is rather appalling. If you live in the farm districts, and note the teams that pass, you will be apt to see the farmer on foot ; and his horse panting, with lowered head, follows dejectedly after, dragging the wagon. The vehicle itself has its wheels so balled with snow that the spokes are almost filled in between, while the hubs have swollen ponderously, and the rims are ten times their natural size. That the snow takes the frost out of the ground seems to be past argument, when one notes the effect of its melting. How else could the mud be so vastly augmented?

A March Roadway

65

There is no feature, perhaps, of the changing seasons that impresses the observer more at this time of year than the effect of spring on the roads. For from four to eight weeks the travel-

A Highway in Time of Flood

ling is, to say the least, something much better talked about than experienced. First, in the breaking up of winter the snow softens, and the horses slump through at every step, and your sleigh pitches about like a ship in a heavy sea. Next, the bare earth begins to show in spots, and the muddy roadway is exposed here and there. As a result, the paths of the travellers become characterized by a remarkable irregularity. To take advantage of the snow, vehicles on runners dodge all about the roadway, from this side to that, and often make detours far out into the fields. In every hollow a shallow pond forms, and these sheets of water are by no means lacking even in the main highway. When your

horse takes a lively gait through one of the larger of these roadway ponds, the sensation is much that of a voyage by water on a
little steam-tug.

On the days when the mud is at its worst, a drive along a
country road is much like a drive through a bog as many miles
long as the journey is. The horse can do little but plod ; and, if
the wagon is heavily loaded, it is not unlikely you will find spots
where he cannot do even that. When a teamster finds himself
stalled in the mud he throws off a part of his load, or gets the
driver of some friendly team to hitch on ahead, and pull him out
of his rut. There are times when he has to unhitch his horses,
and abandon the wagon altogether for the time being.

PICKING UP FLOODWOOD

While the mud is at its worst, no team will keep the middle
of the road if it can help itself. If there is turf along the way the

teams take to that ; and soon it is so cut up with wheels, and so hacked to pieces with hoofs, you would not think grass could ever grow there again. In all villages each farmer takes a certain pride in his home lawn ; though, curiously enough, he does not take pride enough in anyone else's lawn to prevent his driving on it if it is unprotected in the spring mud-time. But it is a common habit, as soon as one's turf is threatened, to drag out rails and sticks of cord-wood, and throw here and there along the roadside to encourage the passing teams to stick to the mud. This road-side decoration is not specially ornamental. It looks as if some-one's fence or wood-pile had blown away, but it serves its purpose.

The roads dry unevenly, and often with little apparent logic. But the highway can be depended on to be slowest to settle where sheltered by woods and where the big drifts have longest lingered. Sandy levels are very quickly dried, and the dust flies on them weeks before other parts have arrived at their summer aspect. A wind which does not freeze is heralded as a good thing, "because it will dry up the mud." The harder it blows, the more effective it becomes. A gradual approach of mild weather is also regarded with complacence as regards its relation to mud. It is argued that this allows the frost to subside deep down, so that when the hard winter upper surface is reduced to mud, the layer which must be relieved of frost before the mud will disappear is much thinner than it would be had the thaw been marked enough to make surface mud at once.

It is about the first of April the farmer makes up his mind that winter has come to an end, and that travelling on runners is without question past. Having that thought firmly fixed in his mind, he and one of his sons, or the hired man, put away the sleds for the summer. The careful man winds his Sunday-go-to-meeting sleigh in an old sheet, and perhaps goes so far as to hoist it up on the beams in the corn-house. The man who is not care-ful simply puts the winter vehicles in any place that comes handy, where they will be out of the way till snow flies again, and where they may serve through the warm weather for henroosts, for all the attention he will give them.

In-doors the advent of spring is considered undoubted about the time a fine, quiet day comes, when the mid-day heat is such that fires are no longer needed, and doors and windows can be thrown open with comfort. Mrs. Farmer's mind has been running on house-cleaning for some time past; but this warm day has the effect of clinching things, and she remarks to her daughter that they really must begin the work at once.

Mr. Farmer succumbs to persuasion and mild invective, and finds himself compelled to make up a bucket of white-wash. For two or three days he spends his spare time flourishing a broad brush, wherewith he gives the ceilings of all the rooms of the house a coating that is declared to make the apartments look much better, besides being healthy.

SPRINGTIME

Meanwhile, Mrs. Farmer and her daughter are attacking the rooms, one by one, turning closets inside out and everything else upside down, revelling in soap-suds, and leaving no crack or crevice untouched in the energy of their campaign. Carpets are torn up, and thrown out of the windows; and the men-folks are expected to swing them over a rope strung high in air between two convenient trees, and give them a beating. The children enjoy taking a hand in this beating, and will ply the long apple-tree twigs or the horse-whip with vigor for a time, and take great delight in the puffs of dust which every blow starts; but they have not the strength to keep up the work for such a length of time as is deemed necessary, and they tire of the dust as well as of the labor. Some one older finishes the job, and is always astonished at the amount of dust a carpet can contain, and is heartily thankful, by the time he has finished, that house-cleaning comes but once a year. To be sure there is some pretty vigorous skirmishing with soap-suds and scrubbing-brushes in the fall, but the upheaval stops short of carpets.

After the carpet is cleaned, the men-folks are invited to help put it down. The problem as to whether it is worn so it ought to be turned is discussed and decided, darning or patching done if necessary, and then those engaged crawl around on hands and knees in an endeavor to make the carpet fit snugly, and tack it there. For some days after the affray, evidence of it may be found in the stray tacks which one is liable to encounter, with more or less pain or pleasure, anywhere and at any time.

While this spring renovating is underway, one often feels like a stranger and intruder in his own home. Let the furniture be all askew, and the carpet up, or the pictures and shelf-ornaments all down, and he has difficulty in placing himself. Especially is this so if new wall-paper is to be put on, or the kitchen-floor painted. In the latter case the family moves out of the kitchen for a few days; and what travel is necessary in that room is done on boards laid down on sticks' to connect with the cellar-door, the buttery, and the sink. One imagines himself walking on a narrow bridge above a flood, though the colors — red or yellow — do not stimulate this idea very powerfully.

The sitting-room, for the time, becomes the living-room and the working-room. Even the meals are eaten there. The children, if not the others, enjoy the romance of the change, and feel like visitors in their own house. The only drawback is that they are not allowed to loiter and race on those boards laid down on the kitchen-floor as much as they would like.

The farmhouse with its outbuildings is usually so placed as to form a rough semicircle opening toward the south. This gives a certain protection from winter winds. As a result, the snow disappears from the dooryard a number of days before it does from the surrounding fields; and no sooner is the snow gone than an unpleasant odor becomes apparent in the back-door neighborhood, and shows that the ghosts of the slops it had been found convenient to throw out there during the winter are beginning to assert themselves. Mrs. Farmer, thereupon, declares that the yard has got to be cleaned up.

After the cleaning, the odors subside to a degree; but then follow some days or weeks when the earthy portion of the yard is characterized by a general bogginess, which necessitates the laying down of lines of boards to such points as it is absolutely necessary to reach.

The hens become an interesting feature of the scene about this time. They have spent most of their time during the winter meditating and picking about on the barn-floor, or the immediate vicinity, varying the programme with sundry excursions to the back steps, where they are fond of sunning themselves, and where they may frequently pick up a stray crumb, or find a swill-pail to dip into. The back piazza and adjoining steps are forbidden territory on most farms; and Mrs. Farmer is liable to appear

THE SPRING FRESHET

at any moment with a broom and some ejaculations that the hens seem to understand as particularly frightful, for they scurry away in great consternation. Nevertheless, they show little hesitation in making other visits when the coast is clear.

AFTER FLOOD TRASH

Now that the snow has receded, the hens make little expeditions along the base of the house, and nip off the first green spears of grass that appear, and doubtless find other things pleasing to their palates. Their joy becomes complete when they find a spot that is sufficiently dry so that they can scratch and wallow in it, and make the dust fly.

Of course the model farmer keeps his hens in a hen-house, and depredations of this sort are bygones; but the majority of our country people are not model farmers yet.

As soon as the nights are no longer frosty, and the ground becomes once more earth and not mud, the farmer concludes it is time to plough his garden. The first exercise preparatory to this is the trimming up the broken limbs of the apple-trees about the place, and perhaps the cutting off dead limbs and "suckers," with the refuse of which he makes a bonfire. If the farmer or any of his family has a touch of the poetic or the romantic instinct, this ceremony is deferred till evening, when the leaping flames and the flying sparks, and the figures in sharp relief of light and shadow, make a spectacle well worth looking at and being a part of.

WHIPPING OUT A FIRE

The day following certain loads of a fertilizing nature, which one would best keep to windward of, are conveyed from the barn-yard to the garden patch ; and by nightfall the little field has been ploughed, a strip where the onions are to go raked over, and a couple of rows of potatoes and four rows of pease planted. The whole family goes out and takes part in the work for a while after supper ; and when the darkness deepens, and brings their labor to a close, they still loiter a while to have the satisfaction of a short contemplation of this work, so well begun.

Long before, even when the snows of early March were fly-ing, Mrs. Farmer had started some tomato-plants in-doors. She planted the seeds in such wooden boxes as she could find, in tin pots, earthern pots, old tea-cups — nothing, in fact, came amiss. She kept them during the day on the window-sills with a sunny exposure, starting with the window-sills in the east in the morning, and ending in the evening with those in the west. At night this array of pots and boxes reposed on the shelf behind the stove.

It may be observed that, in with the tomatoes, the smallest children of the house had begged to insert a variety of other seeds, such as onion, pumpkin, and cucumber. They "just wanted to

WASHING UP FOR DINNER

see how they would grow," and when these became troublesome they were pulled out.

Tomatoes have delicate constitutions, and it is not till some time after the garden was started that they are transplanted to it. Even then each plant has a shingle stuck up beside it to protect it from the noonday sun, and is watered regularly for several days.

Now that the garden has been started, spring on the farm may be said to be fairly under way, and things begin to settle down to their ordinary warm weather routine.

I suppose that in the general satisfaction that is felt over the fact that winter is past, the country dwellers can take the hard travelling and omnipresent mud philosophically and with little of complaint. But when the warm, dry days of May come, with the green grass and blossoms, and new leafage in the orchards and in the wood lands, no season of the year is hailed with more delight.

V

BACK–DOOR NOTES

THE front of a farmhouse rarely undergoes any change. I do not count the gradual wearing away of the paint, and the occasional restoration of faded tints by fresh applications. I grant, too, there are exceptions, as in cases where the proprietors are inspired to adorn the front of the house with a new porch, piazza, or a bay window. But occurrences of the latter nature are comparatively rare ; and as a rule the house is, to the passer-by, the same old house year in and year out.

It is not so with the rear of the premises. If one will keep watch there, he will find change continual. A farmer seldom has room enough for his stock and crops, and his wagons and tools, so that everything is handy and to his liking. He always feels the need of an extra shed or two ; and if he finally gets that extra shed or two, he finds, after all, that he ought to have one or two more. When the need seems imperative, and there is not time or money for anything more elaborate, he builds a lean-to out of such boards and slabs as he can pick up about the place.

Nearly every winter the farmer takes a few logs to mill, and has them sawed into boards and plank for his own private use.

He stows them under the barn, or on the beams in one of the sheds, where they may be handy against a time of need.

Beside the fresh boards stored, there are quantities of second-

BACK-DOOR PETS

hand material and odds and ends set up in convenient corners all about the rear farm-buildings, both inside and out. It is not easy to say just where all this rubbish comes from; but there it always is, and if at times it suffers depletion on the occasion of some building operation, this is only temporary.

The average farmer is pretty sure to have a shop on his premises, where he keeps a variety of the more common carpenter's tools; and when circumstances call for a tool he has not, he can usually

FEEDING THE HENS

borrow it of some neighbor. The borrowing habit is a prominent characteristic of the small farmer, and the neighbors are many of them as well acquainted with a man's shop as the owner is himself. They borrow tools, vehicles, horses, harnesses, — indeed, almost everything, even to a half-day's use of the hired man. Once in a while there is a farmer who has such a thorough familiarity with a neighbor's premises, that he treats them almost as if they were his own, and on occasion he will borrow without the formality of asking. Some men rarely return a borrowed tool, but allow the owner to come after it when he needs it for himself; and there are instances where the borrower keeps the tool so long he forgets it has another owner. He may go so far as to cut his initials on it.

The workroom where the farmer keeps his carpenter's tools could fairly be called " The Old Curiosity Shop." It is a rusty, cobwebby place, with walls and ceiling hung thick with relics of the past. Quantities of other relics and rubbish are scattered about the floor. A good share of these accumulations in the shop are broken, or are stray parts of some article which has gone to pieces. This stuff is kept here partly because the shop serves as a catch-all for things that are in the way elsewhere, partly with the idea that these broken bits may come handy when something else breaks, and repairs are needed.

As a matter of fact, things are always breaking or coming to pieces on the farm, and visits to the shop to find the wherewith to make whole or serviceable the thing broken are very frequent. The shop is in particular a place of resort on days of storm. Such days give an excellent opportunity to tinker and make repairs, or perhaps to wash the farm harnesses, or build a new hen-coop.

Hen-coops, it may be said, always assume importance with the advent of spring; and at that time the agricultural paper taken by the farmer gives considerable space to explaining and illustrating desirable ways to build these domiciles. The simplest method is to make a coop by nailing two boards together in the shape of an inverted V, and then tacking on slats across the sides. In the main, a man will confine his efforts to this style of architecture ; but at times he ventures on the more elaborate schemes suggested by the papers, or works out an idea of his own.

On some farms the hens take care of themselves as far as their place of abode is concerned ; but on many places they not only have their regular quarters, but these quarters are changed, made over, or tinkered, yearly. A new shanty is built for them, or it is partitioned, a chimney put in, or the yard is extended, or a new fence put up around it. If the hen-yard is surrounded by a slatted wooden fence, that fence is continually needing repairs, or some hen develops unusual powers of flight and flies over. Then

THE FARM COLT

is it decreed that the fence must have an upper story put on it, or else it must all be torn down, and some of this new kind of wire fencing, that is advertised, must be bought to put in its place. Even that fence does not attain the perfection that was expected of it, but requires a line of foot-boards to protect it at the base, and sometimes a bristling rampart of lath along the top to keep in the high-fliers.

A good deal of temporary building and fencing in a small way is done on some farms. Has the farmer a small family of pigs? He considers if he cannot build a little hovel for them "somewhere out back," on the grass. Or he thinks it will be a good idea to pen in some calves in that neighborhood, or, it may be, a colt and its mother. After the structures erected have served their purpose, it commonly happens that they are allowed to take their own course in tumbling to pieces. The process is assisted by the farmer himself, who makes their ruins depots of supply whenever other building projects suggest themselves.

Such things as these give to the rear of a farmer's premises a picturesque abandon which is often in striking contrast to their appearance from the road. The rear buildings are usually unpainted — at least the newest and smallest of them are; and their tints, therefore, vary all the way from the yellowest of new pine boards to the brownest and most weatherworn aspect that sun and storm and time can give.

The modern farmer who can afford it, if he be not too economical in his inclinations, paints his barn red when he builds new; but most barns go unpainted from the day they are put up to the time they fall to pieces. Not only is this unpaintedness of the rear view marked as regards the outbuildings, but it frequently extends to the house itself. I do not refer so much to the houses which were last painted a half-century or more ago, nor to those, both ancient and modern, which never were painted. It is to the type of house that has the three sides painted that are in view from the road, but whose gable end, on the fourth side, is left to the tender mercies of the elements.

The farmers do much of their own shingling, painting, and repairing, although there are always two or three men in town to be had who are very good carpenters or painters. But your real Yankee farmer is a jack-of-all-trades, and can do these things fairly well himself. Nor does he always have the money to hire the work done ; and whatever the state of his finances, it is not his habit to make expenditures rashly and without due deliberation.

Another thing to be noted is that he never likes to shingle until it is absolutely necessary. Accordingly, he periodically arms himself with a few shingles, a hammer and nails, and, with a rope swung from chimney or ridgepole, makes zigzagging excursions over the roofs to patch the leaks. In some cases this patching process continues for many years, and the roof becomes amazingly rough in texture and varied in tone.

Occasionally there is a man who, when he shingles, leaves the foot-boards up, and does not trim off the ends of the last row of shingles, which, therefore, are left projecting several inches beyond the peak of the roof. I suppose the explanation of this bristling peak is that the old ridge-boards were worn out, and the man has no proper material at hand with which to replace them. He puts off the getting of them till a more convenient season, and leaves the roof-stagings up that he may get to the ridge handily ; but the seasons come and go, and that "more convenient season" never arrives.

If in what has been described there are hints of shiftlessness or of over-close economy, it is to be remarked that these things are incidental, not general, characteristics. Furthermore, it may be affirmed that the boy brought up on a farm where, from necessity or habit, a somewhat vigorous economy is practised, has a much better chance to win success in life than he who is brought up under milder conditions. As to the aspect presented to the eye by the farmer's unconventional methods of building, much of it is very charming, poetically and artistically considered. Nor, in the main, is it offensive as a matter of thrift.

VI

FINANCIERING ON A SMALL FARM

FARM people have about the same money experiences as other people. There is a difference only in details. The channels by which money comes are few, and are distinctly circumscribed. The ways to spend money are endless, and the wants are sure to outrun all ordinary possibilities of income.

The farm people often figure on what they would do if they had a million dollars ; but no farm people of my acquaintance have ever become possessed of such a fortune, and I do not know positively what they would do if chance brought it their way. When they have a few hundreds fall to them, they apply it to the farm mortgage, or, if there is no mortgage, they spend a small fraction of the money for something they have particularly wanted for a long time, and put the rest in the bank.

A man with money at interest has some standing in the community, and can take some pride in himself ; while it is a good deal of a bugbear to most to have interest to pay, and work a farm with a mortgage on it. There is much reason in this ; for many a farmer who assumes a debt, or has one bequeathed him with his farm when he is young, still has that debt hanging over

him when he is old.   Others, who finally become free owners of
their land, have to drudge with all their families half a lifetime
to accomplish this end.

HIS OWN HOUSEKEEPER

The small farmer sells butter, eggs, an occasional fowl, garden
truck, and apples and other fruit.   He usually does not raise
much of any one thing, and the money comes in driblets.   Most
of the land is given up to hay and corn ; but that is fed out to the
horses and cows, and the money return is in the shape of a small
amount received weekly from the sale of butter.   The attempt
is frequently made to increase the family income.   Schemes
with that end in view are apt to be thought of in the winter.

Things are dull then, and large plans are made for the next season's work. It is easy to dream dreams; but, when it comes to the work, it costs to make them real, and the feeling as to what is possible and desirable changes. Work crowds, the hot days come, and enthusiasm melts with the snow on the fields. Even if a man does raise an extra lot of chickens, or is first with his pease in the market, it is hard for the family to realize that they have handled any more money than usual, for it goes about as quickly as ever. One or two seasons of effort in a particular direction is usually enough, even if the experiment is fairly successful. The man tires of it, and relaxes into the former monotony, or turns to something still newer.

It is the idea on a farm that it is possible to keep a dollar bill a

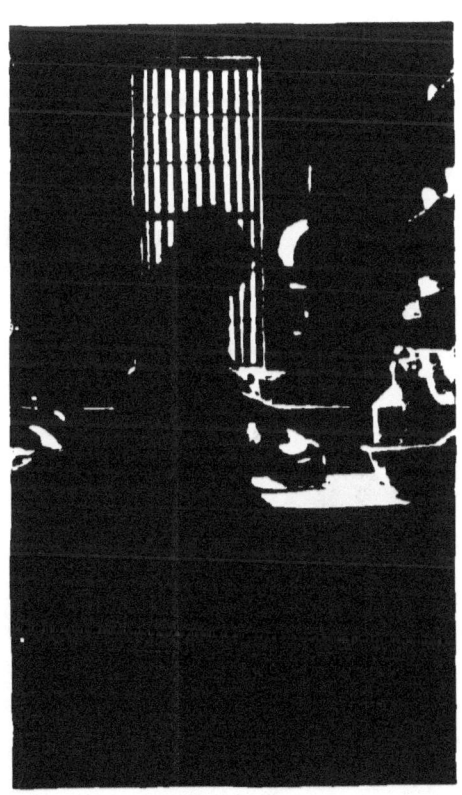

WORKING OVER BUTTER

long time, but that ninety-nine cents is bound to melt away at once, and most unaccountably. Break a bill, and the change is soon spent. Once they have a bill, many of the farm people treasure it, and only break it as a last resort.

It is supposed, too, that it is comparatively easy to pay day by day for what you buy, but that an account allowed to run a few months, or even a few weeks, is extremely difficult to catch up with, and that it is bound to be much larger than you had any idea it would be. Of course, when the bill is presented, the daily wants continue just the same; and to raise the money to cancel the bill, there has to be extra scrimping, or else a larger portion of the farm produce must find immediate market. But there is another way to meet the debt; that is, to pay a little on the bill and keep it running. Probably the account system is not economy for our farmers. They buy what they want when they have it charged. Otherwise they buy what they can pay for. If they have a dollar and a half, they can patronize the butcher on his weekly or semi-weekly visit liberally. If they have only twenty-five cents, they have to select with great care.

TRADING WITH THE BUTCHER

Some kinds of meat will go a long way, and by sticking to bread - and - milk suppers, and toast and griddle - cake b r e a k - fasts, they can get through a great many days without having much to do with the butcher. There is always the farm itself to draw from in the case of a money pinch. If they can't afford to buy from the butcher this week, they can use an extra number of home eggs, and cook one of the old hens. Very likely these things would have sold readily for more than would have been paid for meat, but that phase of finance does not often present itself. The feeling is that what they use off the farm instead of buying is so much clear gain.

Whenever an expenditure is made outside of the every-day routine, it is supposed this must be made up by economy in some other direction. If Mrs. Farmer has a new dress made, then she must make the old hat do for another season, and do without other things she wanted. She tries to buy less meat and groceries, and may even spread her bread extra thin for a time, or do without butter altogether. Mr. Farmer economizes, too, but he does not come down to quite so fine a point as butter. He is fond of butter ; and he only does without it when, accidentally or otherwise, there is

SOMETHING GOOD COOKING

none on the table. Likewise he puts two teaspoonfuls of sugar into his coffee, no matter how high the price of that article is, nor how certain his wife is, when possessed of the economizing spirit, that one spoonful is enough.

There is always some one thing that a farm family which is at all progressive wants. As soon as they get that thing they begin to feel the need of something else. They want a new stove, or a new pump, or a new carriage, or an organ, a carpet, or something of the sort. In order to get the particular thing they happen to aspire to, they are apt to begin saving. They lay aside a dollar or two at a time, and use smaller amounts for expenses. But this method is uncertain; for, like enough, in the midst of the saving something else presents itself that must have the money, or Mrs. Farmer and her daughter are impressed

BOILING THE CLOTHES FOR THE WASH

with the idea that they are getting shabby, or out of style, and absolutely must go shopping. That wrecks the money hoard, and the family has to begin again. If they ever get enough to pay a half or a third down, they buy the thing longed for, and pay the rest a few dollars at a time. They anticipate taxes in the same way. For a month or two before the bill comes they are laying by something to pay on it; but they rarely have enough to cancel it at once, and they meet it, as they do all their large bills, on the instalment plan.

Some families get the notion that the way to become rich is to be systematic and keep accounts. They talk it over; and all of them, from the father to the small boy, are interested, and catch rosy gleams of fortune. They hunt up a little blank book with advertising on every other page; and Mr. Farmer sharpens a new one-cent lead-pencil, and they all look on while he writes some headings. Then the blank book and the pencil are put on the corner of the kitchen shelf; and after that they put down the number

WASHING DAY

of eggs the hens lay each day, and everything they buy. Each member of the family shares in the writing, and what one forgets some one else is pretty sure to remember. The interesting time comes at the end of the month, when they all put their heads together, and reckon up the expenses for that month. The figure columns are a little straggling, and the entries are in several different styles of handwriting; but, by dint of a little puzzling and arguing, the accountants reach a result they can all agree on. Perhaps the family of four or five have spent as much as thirty dollars that month, in which case they are rather appalled, and go back over the lists to see what the leaks have been, and they determine to bring the amount down under twenty the next month. These figures would be too low an average for the year around, and of course they do not charge themselves for what they get off the farm; but except when there is an unusual expenditure for a mowing-machine, a new piazza, a distant visit, a set of chamber furniture, or some of the other extras that people are likely to be taken with longings for, they think it no hardship to get along on twenty or thirty dollars a month on a small farm. The account-keeping has never brought sudden wealth to any of the small farmers, so far as I know; but it tends toward thrift, and is a good thing as far as it goes.

MONDAY

VII

THE VACATION COUNTRY

IN one's imagination the country is very easily idealized. A vacation among the New England hills has its pleasures, but it is not one continual round of unalloyed delight. It is but a small fraction of the time that one's soul is thrilled by either the beauties of the skies or of the fields. As for discomforts, there is no place on earth where a man can get away from them altogether. Yet, if you take such of these vacation discomforts as you chance to meet with in the right temper, you will find that they give your two weeks or more a not unpleasant spin on the whole.

If you like riding or walking, a rambling tour through the country, where you find each night a new stopping-place, will give you the largest returns in enjoyment and pleasant memories. If you settle down at some particular place, your touring must be less varied; though, if you make a study of it, you will discover at least a score of pretty drives in the vicinity. Of course you will go fishing over and over again, and perhaps will try your hand at hunting. Then the life of the town, the home life of the people, and their out-door work about the fields, have many

possibilities of interest ; and if you are not too overpowering in
your style and too esthetic in your tastes, you will find much
to sympathize with in the thought and habits of these country
dwellers.

FISHING

There is something very interesting and pleasurable about the
quiet of a country village in its sleepy days of sunshine, its dull
days of rain, its lack of movement and noise, and its blank lone-
liness after nightfall. To a man in the right mood, who comes
from the ceaseless rattle and business strife of the city, all these
phases of country quiet are restful and refreshing.

The country town I last became acquainted with is typical
enough to be described with some detail. It is eight up-hill miles

A COUNTRY ROADWAY

from the nearest railroad station, nearly all this way through the
woods. The central village is built on what is apparently the
highest hill-top in the township. You sight it while still afar off ;
and the hill looks wonderfully large and steep, and the houses
and the church so marvellously small that they suggest the little
painted blocks of a toy village. There are apple orchards about
the houses, and other orchards cling to the slopes of the hill.
Stone walls divide the fields, and frequent shoulders of the un-
derlying rock crop forth amid the mowing. Indeed, these ledges
reaching out into the open air are almost omnipresent. The man
who can find an acre free from them rejoices as though he had
found a pearl of great price, and will spend weeks with his ox-
team rooting out and carting off ton after ton of the loose stones
and bowlders that encumber the soil. The village on the hill
consists of a white church, a white town hall, a number of white
farmhouses, and several gayer or more gloomy dwellings, both old
and new. One handsome spreading villa is the summer home
of one of the great manufacturers of the country, who some
seasons hardly stays there a full week. Two or three fine old
mansions neighboring are likewise summer homes, and are occupied by families that have become well-to-do in the cities, and
to whom these homes have fallen by inheritance. On a side
street, in a sombre-painted old farmhouse, lives for three summer
months a famous poet, writer, and preacher, who believes this
particular town to be favored by nature above any for at least
fifty miles about.

Among the rest of the hill-top buildings are one or two summer cottages, the doctor's house painted yellow, the parsonage
painted blue, and the two-story school-building painted brown.
It seemed to me the white buildings looked best ; for, in color,
the bright hues were too gay, and the dark ones too gloomy, for
this quiet country village.

The town, a few years back, had right in the centre a big

white tavern, where the post-office and store used to be ; but the building burned down, and the keeper of the tavern moved away. The merchant built for himself a combination store and dwelling on a side street, and had bay-windows put in, and painted the structure brown.   He does not allow smoking, and is inclined to strictness with loafers, so that this particular country store has lost most of the time-honored features of such places.

There is not much going on about town, as far as outward

THE BLACKSMITH

noises and bustle are concerned.   If you live there awhile, you will probably fall into the habit of trying to make it convenient to step to the window every time you hear a team go past.

There is no movement on the street so humble but that it offers an interesting opportunity for conjecture as to what may be the business or pleasure on which the driver is bent. You may see in the morning several farm teams, with butter-boxes and an

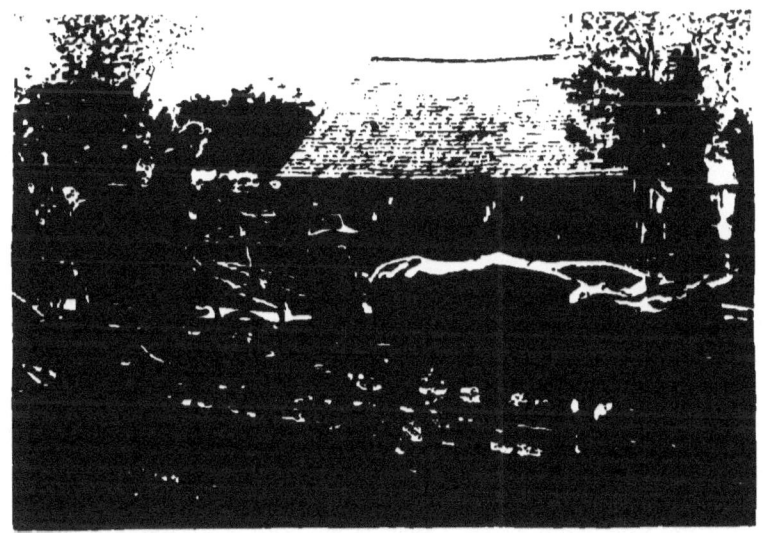

AN OX TEAM

assortment of vegetables back of the seat, on the way to market. Then a boy goes past leading a horse. Probably he is on the way to the little roadside shop of the blacksmith. Now you hear a team rattling along at so lively a gait that you almost have to run to get to the window before it is beyond sight. Ah! that was the Jenkins's city boarders in that smart livery team they hired down in Millington. While you are at the window you see an ox-cart, loaded with hay, drive on the scales up where the sign-board is, at the corners; and Deacon Cook, the storekeeper, comes out, and unlocks the weight-box with his key, and puts on his spectacles to see that he weighs right. The deacon is a very

careful man. They say he will break a cracker in two rather
than cheat you or himself, when he is balancing the scales for the
pound you ordered. After the load of hay drives on over the
hill, you notice Mrs. Smith, with a shawl over her head, walking
across the road to call on Mrs. Jones. She does not stay long,
and she carries a dish with a napkin over it when she returns.
Probably she has been to borrow something in the grocery line.
Country women often make calls of that sort on their nearest
neighbors.

Before you leave the window you see old Mr. Cobb hobbling
along the sidewalk with his cane. He is a very old man, — let
me see, is it ninety-two or ninety-three ? — but he can read without glasses yet. It must be he is going to get last night's paper.
Well, it's no use waiting to see him come back ; for he'll just as
like as not stay there in the store half the day, reading his paper
and talking with the deacon.

The great event of the day is the afternoon return of the
stage. The driver has two or three or half a dozen passengers
aboard. He has brought the papers and the letters, and bundles
of dry goods, and, I'm afraid, bottles of wet goods too, tor the
thirsty of this temperance town. He has done errands to the
number of a dozen or two, and interested parties have been loitering around on the store-steps for a half-hour, at least ; and from
this time on, there is much coming and going in the store neighborhood, both on foot and in teams. The stage still has a long
journey before it, and will hardly get home before dark. The
driver knows this, and he hops about in a very lively manner for
an old gentleman. He hastens back to his place on the front
seat, gives his horses a crack apiece with the whip, and is off.

But these sensations in the village centre should not keep you
from wandering in the fields. There are high pastures to be
visited, where you can look off to the very ends of the earth, or
could if it had any ends. The scrubby slopes sweep down into

the wooded valleys, and, beyond, the blue hills pile on each other, till, in the dimmest distance, they meet the sky. It makes the world look very large.

Nearly all the fences are stone walls, and most of the walls have a wild hedge of briers and bushes growing along them. Some farmers are sufficiently thrifty to keep the bushes out, and the walls in good repair; but such are shining exceptions. One might think that these stone walls would stand forever; but the winter frosts and spring thaws tilt and topple them, and keep them gradually settling into the ground. As for the hedges in their vicinity, it will be worth your while to investigate them. You may be pretty sure there will be some berries to your taste in the tangles. You can take your choice of blackberries and huckleberries, and you can lengthen the bill of fare with choke-cherries and birch-bark and wintergreens.

WASHING THE DISHES

The roads on the hills are peculiarly interesting, both in themselves and in their surroundings. The main roads travelled by the stages are kept in the best repair, and are the least pictur-

esque. The road-scraper, with four horses attached, and two men
to engineer it, goes over the road each year, and rounds it up a
trifle, so that by a little stretch of the imagination you can fancy
it to be turnpiked. A gang of men follows the scraper ; and they
visit with each other, and fill up such holes as they find, and throw
to one side, to be scraped up next year, such bowlders as they
judge will impede travel too much. One of the party carries
an axe, and lops off the roadside bushes that reach too far into
the path.

A man had better think twice before he travels over these

TETHERING THE CALF

roads in winter or in mud-time. He will be apt to lose his
temper, even if he does not otherwise come to grief. In summer
they are quite pleasant. Much of the way they are shadowed

by the woods, they are little cut up by travel, and in the dryest
time you will have but little trouble from dust.   In the wooded
stretches they are usually pleasantly moist and cool.   The border-
ing woods incline to monotony.   They are almost always thick

THE WELL-SWEEP AT THE BACK DOOR

young growths of saplings on land cut off not many years back.
The patches of tall woods that one encounters at long intervals
are very refreshing.

When you take a side road, you do not go a great way before
you find the grasses creeping snug up to the roadway, and a little
farther on you come on stray patches of grass within the wheel
tracks.   Presently these patches become two continuous ridges,
and the horse trots along between them.   Some roads dwindle
into mere lanes that are altogether grass-grown ; and, in many
places, the bushes and scrubby apple-trees fairly arch the path,

and keep up a continual brushing on the sides and top of your
carriage. These side roads have rocks and bumps in them, and
remarkably steep pitches up and down the little hills ; and you are
liable to meet a calf tethered to a roadside sapling, that on your approach runs wildly to the end of its rope straight across the path.

Not a few of these grass-grown byways were once well travelled, and had many houses linked along them. Everywhere are
remnants of orchards, old cellar-holes, and the crumbling ruins of
long-deserted homes. The majority of the houses still inhabited
are ancient and weather-worn, and the farm-life has many of the
simple characteristics of that of fifty years ago. The picket or
quarter-board fences that have become very rare in the valley
towns are still common. Refuse and unsightly litter are prominent in the home surroundings ; and great heaps of manure
thrown out of convenient barn windows are frequent foreground
features of the landscape, as viewed from the house.

A well-sweep in the dooryard is not unusual ; and it is to-day
possible to find, in Western Massachusetts, log houses inhabited,
an open kitchen fireplace still in use, and a household where the
wool for all the yarn that is knit into stockings and mittens for its
members is prepared and spun in the home. In nearly every
town is a woman who has a loom in a chamber or back room, on
which she weaves the rag carpets for the neighborhood ; and, if
you ride through the hill towns in the spring, you will see now
and then a great kettle swung over a fire in the back yard, and
the women of the household busy making soft soap.

One would think that the people in some of these lonely and
shaky old farmhouses were in the direst depths of poverty. But
this is not always the case, even though the whole family is
ragged, and the men's clothing is more patches than original
cloth, and in-door comforts and amenities are almost lacking.
There are those of this class who are putting money in the savings-bank right along.

MAKING SOFT SOAP

Sunday is one of the most interesting days of the country
week.   Quiet broods over the hills year in and year out ; but on
Sunday morning the quiet is so exaggerated you would think all
the people had moved away.   At nine o'clock the church bell
rings, and its peals go echoing far over the fields and pastures.
But there is not a whit more stir on the street than there was
before.   It is simply a reminder to the inhabitants that the Sabbath has come, and a warning to prepare for church.

A second bell rings at half-past ten ; and then people in their
Sunday best begin to appear on the street, headed toward church,
and from every approaching road come the teams of those who
live at a distance.   Buggies and two-seated market-wagons are
the most common among the vehicles that drive up to the high
church-steps to discharge their loads.   There is a hum of visiting
about the front doors and the hall within that knows no intermis-
sion till the bell tolls and the minister comes.   Then the last
woman rustles into her seat, the doors are closed, and the little
organ in the gallery pipes up with Old Hundred.

But I do not need to dwell further on the day here, for the
chapters following describe the Sunday services of a country
church in detail.

VIII

A HILL-TOWN SABBATH

"MEETIN' begins at one o'clock," said my landlady. "We used to have meetin' in the mornin' when we had a settled minister, but that was three years ago or more. Now we have that new man down at Factory Holler. He drives up, after he gets through down there, every Sunday. We can't support a settled minister any more. Those that go pay what they can, and then there's a church fund that Martha Williams left that brings in something. That fund can't be used only for church doings, you know.

"They're all gone, pretty much — all the old families that used to support the church ; and they don't get any such congregation as they used to get. Land ! I've seen that church full many a time, gallery and all. But you take it a stormy Sunday, and nowadays there ain't enough comes to fill two pews. There's plenty to go, though, if they only would go. They've kind o' got out o' the habit o' church-goin', someway, and don't take much interest — they'd ruther laze around home. I don't go myself ; but that's because I ain't got no horse, and I'm gettin' too old to walk so fur."

A little before one o'clock I set out alone for the church. It was a soft, lowery spring day. Bobolinks were singing in the meadows, swallows were twittering about the eaves of the barns. At the houses I passed, the men-folks were sitting on the piazzas, or were wandering half aimlessly about the yard and near fields. Usually they were dressed in their Sunday best; but that was because it was not a work-day, not because they had intentions of going to church.

The meeting-house was a building of goodly size on a low hill-

GETTING READY TO PLOUGH

top. Little valleys and undulating farming-land were all about, and beyond these were wooded hills. The church was, of course, painted white; and it had a pointed spire, green blinds, and at its

rear that invariable accompaniment of the country church, a line
of rickety horse-sheds.

The front door was open when I approached, and on the door-
step a boy was loitering. Near him, in the yard, stood a stoop-
shouldered young man, with withered features, half-shut eyes, and
open mouth. I asked him if there was to be a Sunday-school that
day. He made no reply, and gave no indication that he even
heard me. I repeated the question, and the result was no better.
It was plain that he was one of those whom the country people
speak of as "luny." I turned to the youngster on the steps,
and received an answer in the affirmative. Then I entered the
church. Directly within the door was an "entry" that extended
the full width of the front. Here were three or four small boys.
At either side a stairway led to the galleries, and in one corner
was a small pile of wood. Down the middle of the entry hung
the bell-rope.

The main room beyond had a box-stove in each back corner,
that sent a long span of stove-pipe far across to the wall opposite.
I sat down on an old hair-cloth sofa by one of the stoves, and
awaited developments. The walls of the room had been recently
painted in a pleasant yellow tone. The galleries were partitioned
off from sight, but that they were there was evident from the
rows of columns supporting them. At the farther end of the
room was the low pulpit, with its black-walnut desk, and back of it
an ornamental square of papering. The pews were white with
brown trimmings. They were doubtless furnished by the parties
who occupied them ; for no two were carpeted alike, and in some
the board flooring was entirely uncovered. Two rows of pews at
the rear were slightly higher than the rest, and in a narrow open
space before them was a small cabinet organ.

When I first entered, the room was occupied by an elderly
man, his wife, and two young women. They had started a fire in
one of the box-stoves. It did not go very well, and the old gentle-

man had opened the stove-door to poke it. That let the smoke out. He was not a whit disturbed, and continued to poke till his women-folks began to exclaim, and to insist that he should stop

PLOUGHING

operations at once and shut the door. He was a very mild and amiable old gentleman, and he meekly did as he was bid.

Next he brought in a ladder from the entry, climbed high up to a clock on the rear wall, and wound it with a resonant clicking. While he did this two of the women spread a communion-table in front of the pulpit from a large basket, and after arranging and adjusting things to their satisfaction, covered the service with a heavy linen cloth. Meanwhile, the boy I had seen on the steps outside came in, and asked me what time it was by my watch.

"Ten minutes past one," I replied.

"Well," he said, "one o'clock's the time for Sunday-school to begin, so I guess I'd better ring the bell if I'm ever goin' to."

A moment later the bell was tumbling in its tower, and its summons went rolling out over the hills. I stepped into the entry, and found two boys tugging at the rope, and two more looking on. The bell-ringers pulled as hard as they knew how, so that the rope, when it left their hands, might fly high up toward the ceiling. They all seemed to enjoy this Sunday task very much. After the older boys were through, and the bell had stopped ringing, the smallest small boy took hold of the rope to see what he could do. He tugged and tugged, but brought forth not a sound. "I can do it," he said. "I *have* done it." He threw his whole weight on the rope, and tumbled with it to the floor. The reward of his persistence was a feeble twang from the bell. This encouraged him to keep on, and he produced at intervals several melancholy intonations.

When I went inside again, a young woman was arranging a bunch of arbutus in a pulpit vase. Then the wife of the elderly man who had wound the clock got all the occupants of the room together in the back seats, had her husband fix the fire once more, and then delegated him to invite me to join their Sunday-school. I was glad to accept the kindly invitation.

Before we had fairly settled ourselves to work we heard voices in the sheathed-up gallery. "There are those boys up there getting all cobwebs," said our leader; and she forthwith sent for them, and had them brought in.

Our teacher read the opening exercises in tones sounding and oracular; and the elderly man followed with a feeble-voiced prayer, ending with the Lord's Prayer, in which all joined. In this, as in the responsive reading of the lesson, a few voices spoke with audible decision; but most were content with a gentle murmuring, while some of the youngest barely mumbled, and did very well if they got in one distinct word out of ten.

The asking and answering of the routine questions was next in order ; and a middle-aged woman took the two youngest boys into a pew beyond the stove. She sat in the seat in front of this infant class, and turned half-way around and leaned over its back while she asked them the list of questions found on the right-hand page of the quarterly. The boys were either not interested or not very well posted, for the teacher had apparently to answer most of the questions she asked, herself. Conscience free and duty done, at the end of the list she escorted her class back to that in the rear· of the room.

We eight or ten older ones were more given to argument than the youngsters, and held more varied opinions ; but, even so, interest lagged, and the whole exercise was gone through with rather because it was the proper thing to do than because any enjoyment was found in it.

The room was very quiet — so unlike the busy hum of many voices in city and town Sunday-schools. Here was naught but the slow ticking of the clock, the snap and rumble of the fire, and the lonely voices of question and reply. We were not an uneasy class. Even the children did not change position often ; and our smallest member wandered no farther from the proprieties than to recline against his mother while he wound his lesson-paper into a roll to blow through.

While questions were being put, we studied our quarterlies assiduously, and answers were given seriously and solemnly and only after due deliberation. These answers kept very close to what was said or inferred by the quarterly. When a member ventured an opinion outside of the lines there laid down, it was with the tone of daring possible heresy that would very likely be doubted, and called for explanation or defence. There were various attempts to give practical application to the points in the lesson, but they were not very successful. Some concern was expressed for the unsaved, and it was affirmed with great decision

that any person who expected to be saved by good works alone
was sadly deceived. Mention was made of harsh-mannered
"people, with tongues like drawn swords;" but it was deemed
best not to visit wholesale condemnation on them, for there are
'those who are like a chestnut burr — outside are the prickles,
but inside is the meat."

The lesson was cut short to give opportunity to elect officers
for the year ensuing. There were only a handful to take part,
candidates were few, and the election was simplicity itself. Our
teacher had the honor of being chosen superintendent. She

HARROWING

would, without doubt, fill the place faithfully and well; but her
comment was, "Well, I'm sorry!"

"Why?" asked the moderator. "What's the matter?"

"Because I think you could 'a' done better," was the reply.

The other officers were elected ; and each of these made some half-jocose, half-serious remark on the result. That done, we sang a single verse from the quarterly, and scattered to the near pews in readiness for the regular church services. There were

PLANTING CORN

present thirteen women, seven men, and four small boys. The congregation was further increased by one man who came in late.

Several experts in the singing line gathered about the organ, and I thought they did very well. Music in the average country church is apt to drag and drone; but the young woman at the organ put excellent spirit into the hymns, and the choir seconded her efforts admirably.

The minister spoke, without notes, from the text, "What hath

God wrought ?" His manner was not halting, as is often the
case of those who attempt extemporaneous sermons, and he was
neither dismal nor oratorical. The incidents and illustrations, too,
of his discourse were frequent and interesting.

Communion followed the sermon. There was a hush even
deeper than before when the minister laid the cloth aside, and the
bread was broken, and the wine tinkled and gurgled from the nose
of its heavy silver urn, to be distributed by the single bent old
man. The children were particularly intent, and watched everything with wide-eyed interest. A collection was taken up after
the communion ; and its nature, like that gathered in the Sunday-
school, was such that anything but coppers looked lonesome.

All rose to sing the final hymn. Like many larger congrega-
tions, they came up in a scattering, desultory sort of way, as if the
hymn had caught them unawares in a nap or in some profound
cogitations that shut out all worldly routine of the present.

After the benediction, meeting broke up and visiting began.
The clatter of tongues in sprightly talk and exchange of news
was in sharp contrast to the somewhat lugubrious atmosphere of
the service preceding. The tendency was for the women to
gather in the hall, while the men went down to the horse-sheds,
and visited for a longer or shorter time while getting out their
teams. Sometimes a man drove up to the door, and no wife
appeared. Sometimes the woman was ready on the church-steps,
and no man appeared. The waiting woman might go so far as to
look anxiously around the corner toward the sheds for her escort,
but the man who had to wait did not usually disturb himself to
the extent of looking up the delinquent women-folks. He would
sit in his buggy or stand beside it, and await their pleasure. The
gradual dispersion of the congregation at length saw the last of
the nine teams which had been in the sheds jog away down the
road, and the church-door was locked for another week.

When I returned to my stopping-place the meal, which served

for both dinner and supper on Sunday, was being put on the kitchen table.

As I finished my apple-pie at the close of the repast, and prepared to rise, my landlady said, " Well, church was pretty good to-day, I should think from what you say. Mr. Dove's a smart preacher, and it's queer more don't go. Now, if you're goin' to set down to read, you better go into the settin'-room. The windows look right out onto the road, and you c'n see the teams go by from there."

IX

SUNDAY AFTERNOON

THE afternoon that I make the subject of this chapter was spent in a little village in the Green Mountains. The family with whom I was stopping was up to the average in that region, and their conversation and ways were no more rustic than those of a large part of our New England people who happen to be outside the more modern, progressive currents of life.

The household consisted of a stout, middle-aged woman, an old man, and a second woman, who was something of an invalid, and who kept to her room so that I did not see her at all. It was the middle-aged woman who owned the place, and who was at the head of affairs. She said to me, " This old man, here, he ain't my husband. I ain't got no husband. He ain't got no wife. He does my chores. He's eighty-four years old, too old to be good for much, but he c'n do small jobs, and kind of keep things repaired up around. Uncle Gid! you'll have to give the pig some swill. There ain't nothin' else for him. Just lift the kittle off there in the back kitchin'. There ain't no need o' its bilin' all day."

The News

Uncle Gid was a white-bearded, wrinkled old man ; but, in spite of his years, he was still straight, and still retained a certain briskness in his movements. Now he laid aside his newspaper and spectacles, and went out in the back room. At the same time a small boy from the neighbor's came in at the door, without knocking, as is the custom among country people. The boy looked at me for a minute in speechless amazement. He was not used to strangers. Then he asked, " Is aunt Maria here ? "

" You c'n go right into her room," said my landlady. The boy disappeared ; and she continued, " She ain't no more aunt than you be to him. But that's what they all call her round here. She ain't no relation to me neither ; but she has folks out in

A DRINK AT THE END OF THE ROW

Nebrasky, and they pay me so much a week for takin' care on her." I could hear Aunt Maria's complaining voice saying, "Well, I can't go, you know I can't."

"He's askin' her if she don't want his ma to take her to ride, I guess, it's so pleasant. He won't git her though, 'tain't likely. She don't go out more'n two or three times in a whole year. I guess she's talkin' about you now."

"He ain't a minister, is he?" Aunt Maria was saying.

"She's deef; and you can't make her understand, specially mornin's. I was tellin' her you went to meetin', and she's got the idea you might be the minister."

The kitchen in which we sat had a yellow-painted floor, much worn in the middle of the room, so that the color was nearly gone there, and knots and nail-heads stood up prominently. The woodwork of the walls was painted blue, with red striping. In one corner was a desk covered with litter. Above the desk was a bookshelf, on which were two books and a variety of odds and ends; and neighboring that were a newspaper bracket, an insurance calendar, and a large looking-glass. On another shelf stood a tall, dark old clock, ticking meditatively. Under the clock were hung two patent-medicine almanacs. At the opposite side of the room was the dining-table, with a huddle of dishes in the centre of it, covered with pink fly-netting. The room contained three rocking-chairs, three common chairs of the old-time, straight-backed variety, and three of a more gentle type. The stove was on the hearthstone of an old fireplace, that extended well out into the room. Behind it, against the wall, was a high, narrow wood-box, pasted over with wall-paper. The chief features of the long mantel above were its dado of oilcloth and two lamps. On a nail near by were two squares of padded cloth to handle hot things with. The only picture in the room was a small one, of a monkey pulling nuts from a fire with a cat's paw. The frame of the picture attracted my attention. It was covered with putty, which was stuck all over with shells, stones, buttons, silver paper from tobacco packages, suspender buckles, etc. "Where did you get it?" I asked.

"I made it," said my landlady. "Didn't you know I had a little injun?"

"Injun" was her word for ingenuity.

There was no fire in the stove. On it was a dish of apples that everyone was expected to help themselves to. During the warmer months the kitchen, in most homes, is used as a dining-room, and all cooking is done in the back kitchen. Of course, in many houses, there is no back kitchen to move into at the approach of hot weather; and in such households one has to eat in the same sweltering, tropical heat that the cooking is done in. This is not very agreeable for the men, who come in at noon

MENDING THE FIRE

after a whole morning spent in the hot sunshine; and it is harder still on the women, who have had to be over the stove for the past hour or two.

At my stopping-place the back kitchen had much the unfinished, catch-all appearance that such rooms are apt to have. It was a roughly boarded room, with a low brown-beamed ceiling. In the little stove a fire was burning which sent forth a slight snapping and rumbling that one would hardly have noticed except in the quiet of a Sabbath afternoon, when even the buzzing of the flies on the window-panes sounds loud. Thin wisps of smoke escaped from the cracks of the stove, and lent their odor to the air. At the side of the stove was a small red wood-box, with a pair of brass-handled tongs leaning against it. Various things hung behind the stove, — aprons, a dust-pan, an old hat-rack, a tin match-safe ; and there was a shelf with a worn wing and a pair of shoes on it. Near the door was a little sink piled up with kettles and pails, with a towel on the wall handy, and a pot of soft soap on a convenient window-sill. Then there was a bench with a pail of water on it, brought from the spring back of the house. Before the door was a husk mat. In one corner were a broom, a pan of shavings, and a hoe. In another corner were a heap of dirty clothes, a washboard, and a cloth-covered ironing-board. Shelves here and there were nailed to the wall, full of old crockery and odds and ends, and there were lines under the ceiling hung with other odds and ends ; and there were nails in the wall whereon were suspended old vests, baskets, paper bags, etc. Finally there were three upright, splint-bottomed chairs that had seen better days. One of these chairs had a cushion, and on it lay the family cat. She slept there nights, my landlady said.

About half-past two one of the neighbors called. He was a tall, thin man, dressed in his best clothes. My landlady introduced him as a man who "had travelled." "You c'n talk to him about everything," she said ; but I preferred to be a listener. The man took an apple, and sat down in a rocking-chair.

"Heerd how Miss Fadden is to-day ? " asked my landlady.

"Miss Fadden's miserable," said the man. "Doctor Bugby said she would never live to see the leaves turn in the fall."

"She's worked herself to death," commented the other.
"Done all her housework, and worked out o' doors too. What's
Jim doin'?"

"Oh, he's just tinkerin' round the farm there. He ain't never
done what he ought to 'a' done for his wife. Likes to be up in
the mountains skylarkin' around with his gun too well. But he
feels it some since Doctor Bugby says he can't do nothin' for
her."

"You don't believe much in doctorin', yourself, do you,
'Lisha?" questioned my landlady.

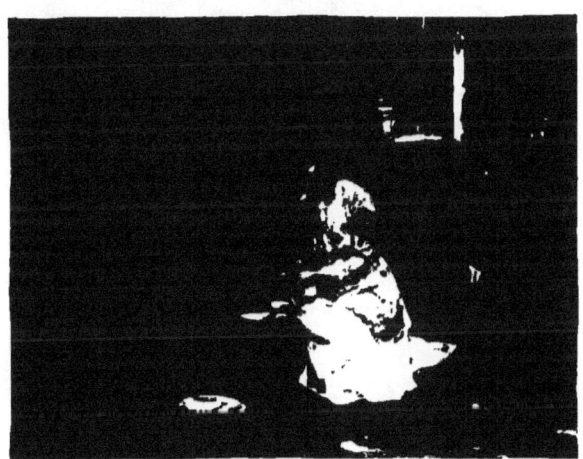

PEELING POTATOES FOR DINNER

"No; if I'd gone to doctors, I'd been in the ground long ago.
I ain't a well man, but I won't have none of these doctors foolin'
round me. You bet I won't stand no such nonsense."

"Waal, doctors don't know as much as they pretend to, I
guess; but you have to have 'em sometimes — in these 'ere kind
of a thing like where there's cutting, you know."

" Yes, that's different. Did you know Martha Spinney was
dead ? "

" I heerd last night. I didn't think she was goin' to die ; I've
seen folks jess so, and they got well. She died sudden at the
last, didn't she ? "

PLANTING WITH A MACHINE

" Yes ; Lord o' macy ! they say she died in a chair. I asked
if she throwed up anything. Bert, he was there when she died,
and he said she didn't."

" I'd nacherly think she would."

" Waal, I guess she did, if truth was told."

The discussion of Martha Spinney's death was prolonged, and
went into details too unpleasant to repeat. The next subject
brought up was the city people, who had built a number of fash-
ionable summer houses in the neighboring town. " Have you
ever been over there where them city folks air ? " asked my landlady, turning to me. " It's over near Rainbow Falls they tell

PARING APPLES

about. I thought mebbe you might 'a' been there. They don't very frequent come by here, but I can tell 'em when they come. They have their barouches, and their negro drivers, and their horses' tails are bobbed right square off. They look different too. Then, sometimes, they come up riding on horseback, and the women have on long habits ; and there's a groomsman follerin' behind, all fixed up in great style — white pants, black coat, and all such fixin's."

" They all go to the 'Piscopal church over there, don't they ? " inquired the visitor.

" Yes, and I went one day too. But what kind o' sense is there in that 'Piscopal service, I'd like to know, — all gettin' up and settin' down, and a long lingo that they go through tight as they can jump. Might just as well set down and hear a pa'cel o' geese. That's my notion o' things."

About this time two other visitors arrived, and Uncle Gid came in with them. They were a young man named Lucius, and his mother, Mrs. Hapwell. They hitched their team to a post outside the gate.

" Hurraw ! " said Mrs. Hapwell. " Here we air. Caught ye at it this time."

" Come in and set down," said my landlady.

" Been lookin' at the dayl-yas (dahlias) along," said the new-comer. " Yours are doin' a sight better'n mine."

" I ain't seen you in a long time," said Elisha. " How are you now ? "

" I ain't in very good health," was the reply, " rather slender. I've worked just like a ole nigger the whole week. Then I went away up into the lot where Fred's workin' a-Friday, and yisterday I was clean beat out. I heard you'd come around again, 'Lisha. Why don't you git married ? "

" Waal, do' know but I will, if you'll find me the girl."

" There's the Tompkinses. It's kind o' hard on the old man

to take care o' the hull on 'em. You must go and spark up the oldest girl. Hetty's fifteen. She thinks she's old enough."

"That's all right, but she ain't got any money. I want to get some one that's got money — I don't care how old she is."

Pretty soon after, Elisha left, and the others went into the sitting-room.

"He wants to get rich all in a minute, don't he?" said Mrs. Hapwell.

Mowing the Home Lot

"Waal," was my landlady's comment, "he must have some-thin' laid up by now. He's been workin' at engines, repairin' on 'em, for a good many years, and he's had big pay. He thinks he may go to farmin' out now. He's a good, likely, stiddy fellow, I calerlate. But he says he ain't well at all."

131

A BOOK OF COUNTRY
CLOUDS AND SUNSHINE

"He eats too much — that's what's the matter with him, by golly!" said Lucius. "If 'twan't for that, he'd be all hunkedory."

"How old is he?" asked Mrs. Hapwell.

"Must be all of forty-five," said my landlady.

"Guess he is," was the response. "Why, Lord, he was goin' to school when I was! Yes, 'Lisha's over fifty to-day. Uncle Gid," said she, changing the subject, "I'm most choked to death for some water; wish the land you'd go and git some."

"Spring's right out north the house," said Uncle Gid jokingly. "You'll find a gourd hangin' on the bush there."

"I'll fix *you*, Uncle Gid," was the lady's reply, as she shook her fist at him threateningly.

"Can't you go and git a pail of water?" my landlady said. "Seem's if you might. I don't want to have to jaw and blow and git mad just to git a pail o' water."

Uncle Gid started; and my landlady continued, "I'm thirsty myself. We had fish for dinner. Always dretful dry stuff, fish is. What you doin' now, Lucius?"

"Waal, been plantin' corn in the meader lot, — that's the last thing. Ain't but a dang few got their corn in yet. Rained like fury last night, didn't it? I vow, I thought it would wash my corn all out."

"Ansel's widow 's goin' to git married," said Mrs. Hapwell.

"No, is she?" was my landlady's response. "Waal, I knew she'd ketch some one. Got Caleb Jackson, didn't she? I heard he was goin' with her some."

"Ma's been paperin' lately," said Lucius.

"Yes," said his mother. "Every room's painted with blue, and I got blue papers to correspond."

"I been makin' soap this last week," said my landlady.

"Have good luck?" asked the other lady. "Lucius," said she, looking out of the window, "what's that horse stompin' so for? You go out and see what's the matter with that plug."

" Guess he thinks we've staid long enough," replied Lucius.
" Waal, I don't know but we have," said his mother. ' " I
told 'em we'd be home airly. You jest get unhitched while
I run in and see how Aunt 'Ria is, and then I'll be along."

I have not reported all the afternoon's conversation ; but these
were real people, and I have kept very close to their real words
and manner. The sitting-room in which they sat during the
latter part of their visiting was low and slightly stuffy. It had
a vertical-patterned wall-paper of light tone, and the woodwork
was a grained yellow. On the floor was a large-figured carpet,
in which red, green, and black were the predominant colors. A
bit of oilcloth before each of the two doors, and a braided rag
mat, and a long strip of rag carpet, protected the most travelled
parts of the room from wear. Two small-paned windows looked
out on the roadway. Before one of them, on a stand, were two
wooden boxes, with young tomato-plants sprouting in them.
On another stand, against the wall, were a Bible, a photograph
album, a lamp, and two pairs of spectacles. There were two
small tables in the room, occupied by several recent copies of a
fashion journal and of a New York story-paper, with a few old
books and magazines. Then there was a sewing-machine, with
a gay patchwork-covered footstool next it, a sofa with a calico
spread, and six old parlor chairs. Besides, there was a single
rocking-chair with a calico cushion. A hanging corner-bracket
held three books, three photographs, and a fancy box ; and a
shelf was adorned with a number of advertising cards and medi-
cine bottles. On the walls were a mirror, a portrait in a deep
black-walnut frame, and six chromos, some in ancient frames,
some simply tacked up. The picture which attracted my attention especially was entitled " Lovers' Happiness." Two doll-
like figures were prominent. The young man was dressed in
blue and red and yellow, and had long hair parted in the middle.
He was on one knee, holding the hand of a girl dressed in white,

who stood before him. Behind the girl was an urn, and in the distance lay a lake. No pains were spared to make the picture entirely gallant, graceful, and romantic. Pictures of this sort are common in their homes; but whether it is because there is a liking for the gaudy sentimentality of them, or because, having wandered into the house, they hate to throw them away, is uncertain. The room had a fireplace originally, but it was now bricked up. " Used to have fireboards put up there that we could take down," said my landlady. " But they'd git afire, so we had the bricks put in."

This sitting-room was a little behind the average in that it had no organ, and in many households there would have been more books. Most families take a daily or a weekly, published at the nearest big town, to keep them posted on neighborhood affairs in all the region round about. Besides, they are apt to take a religious denominational paper, and the *Youth's Companion.* Once in a while some other papers of higher or lower character are taken, and an occasional magazine. There are the Sunday-school and town libraries to draw from, and you can find people who are students and lovers of good literature; but in the main country reading is a hit-or-miss affair, with very little aspiration in it, and the home libraries, in nine cases out of ten, are pretty dismal picking.

Many houses have a shut-up parlor, only opened on company occasions, where all the stiffest furniture and choicest treasures of the house, in the way of vases, pictures, and hair wreaths, are kept. The blinds are always closed on that corner of the house, to keep the sunlight from fading the carpet and the upholstered rocking-chair. It is an apartment to be admired, not used; and, to one not enamoured with that sort of thing, its twilight and close odor, and its unnatural orderliness, are very unpleasant. However, it seems almost a necessity for a human being to have a hobby of some sort; and, if a housewife's mind is not capable of aspiring

to anything better than a shut-up parlor, it is no great matter.
The parlor is harmless, and it is the woman's happiness. But the
tendency now is to turn all rooms into use, and shut-up parlors
are gradually becoming less prevalent.

Sunday afternoon is spent in various ways in different commu-

SUNDAY AFTERNOON

nities and in different households. The visiting described in this
chapter is only one type. In most homes it is a time of dozy
quiet. The older people lay down on the sofa and take a nap, or
fall asleep in the rocking-chair while reading the newspaper ; the
mother reads aloud to the uneasy small children ; the oldest
daughter plays hymns on the organ ; the young man, after an
appropriate length of time spent in his room, prinking, appears in
all the glory of starch and perfumery, and gets out the top-buggy,

and goes to take his girl to ride ; the hired men loaf in the shade
of an apple-tree back of the house.

With the approach of dusk, things take a livelier air, the
languor of the day is in part thrown off, and the evening work
at the barn and about the kitchen begins, while the children are
allowed to run and play a little out-of-doors, if they are not too
noisy about it.

X

A CHRISTIAN ENDEAVOR MEETING

THE church where the Endeavorers met was on a hill-top ; and,
except for those who lived in the few near houses, everyone
had to climb to get there. The time of meeting was seven o'clock.
On the October evening that I was present, I arrived a half-hour
early. The evening was clouded, and it was already dark. Cheerful sparks of light shone from home windows, and glinted through
the blinds of the church. In the hallway that was across the front
of the building was a numerous group of boys and men, some
standing, some sitting on the settees along the walls. This
group usually did its before-meeting visiting on the church-steps.
There they could not only observe with detail all the new arrivals,
but could contemplate them as they approached from afar. However, the wind blew this night too keen and chilling.

In the main room of the church the two stoves in the back
corners were going full blast ; and the heat, in contrast with the
frosty air without, made a thick mist gather on the small, old-time
panes of the windows. Newcomers from the cold outer darkness
always got into the corners by the stoves when they first entered ;
but two or three minutes in that baking heat were usually sufficient,

and then they scattered. Three big lamps hung from the ceiling along the centre of the room, and put the place in a twilight glow. A low gallery ran around three sides of the church, and at the

OPENING THE HAY

back of the gallery some of the earlier arrivals were rehearsing hymns to sing on Monday at a funeral. The walls of the room were papered with an old-fashioned dado, that in the upper parts showed stains of leakage from the roof. At the farther end of the room, in front of the pulpit, were a table and two chairs ; and there the leader of the evening presently took his place. A small organ was in the open space near by, and the leader asked one of the young women of the audience to play it.

There were seventy-five or eighty people present, and they

about filled the central mass of seats in the church. The galleries and the seats under the galleries were vacant. Probably fully as many were present as had been at service in the morning. They were mostly young people, though a few of middle age or past were sprinkled among them.

All through the service there was frequent singing from gospel hymns. Sometimes the leader selected the hymn, but more often members of the audience asked for favorites. Many sang these hymns from memory, without the aid of books. The tunes selected always had an easily caught melody; and the rendering was usually pleasingly simple, and often it was unconsciously pathetic. The hymn-tunes in the morning services in the average country church are apt to be slow-moving and dull, and this makes the lightness and ease of the evening music seem in contrast doubly pleasing.

The leader made two short addresses on the topic of the day; and when he read a selection from the Bible, he made comments on the text as he went along. Most of the young men present wore starched linen and store clothes of comparatively recent purchase, and there was a Sunday slickness apparent about their whole persons. Indeed, one or two had an outward immaculateness and style that would put some of our city youth on their mettle to compete with. But the leader seemed a sort of John the Baptist, who "came not clothed in soft raiment." He had an almost everyday, backwoods bushiness and rudeness of exterior that were quite picturesque and interesting. What he said showed thought and sense. He was very well read in some directions, and I was told he had a fondness for quoting from Homer and from history. He had an impediment in his speech, but this rather added to the rough vigor of his short sentences.

He said: "The subject to-night is, 'How Christ helps in our daily tasks;' or, in other words, how religion helps, how hope helps. It don't matter whether you run an engine, keep a store, teach school, or farm it, religion ought to help you. I believe in

HAVING TIME

a practical religion. Unless religion can help us in our tasks, it
can't at any other time."

Several men and several women spoke or prayed, or repeated
verses of Scripture or of hymns. The prayers of the men were
usually plain and straightforward. In one of the prayers a bit of
poetry was quoted. I thought it came in very effectively, but I
learned later that it was quite offensive to some of those present.
They could stand almost anything but praying to God in poetry.
The women were less clear than the men in what they said, and
their speech was inclined to be light-voiced to a degree that
approached inaudibleness.

Between the closing remarks of one member and the opening
ones of another, there were apt to be solemn silences, in which the
ticking of the clock, uneasy rustlings among the children, and a
slight crackling from the stoves, were very apparent.

The leader had distributed a number of paper slips with
questions on them among the members, and the replies to these
occupied a part of the time. I make some quotations from what
was said.

A woman spoke thus: "Christ doesn't change a bit. He's
always the same. He's just the same on Monday as he is on
Sunday. I'm glad I can sing to-night, —   ·

' I have entered the valley of blessing.'

Christ is the light of the world. If there's one here to-night that
knows not that light, I wish he would open his heart now, this
very hour, and let it in. He's knocking at your door. He's waiting still for you. Oh, could you treat any earthly stranger as
you treat him — keep him always waiting outside your door? All
you've got to do is to say, ' Yes, Lord,' and he will let you in.
Get that salvation, so freely promised, in your heart. You have
no friend on earth so dear to you as him. Why don't you let

him come in? Why always keep him waiting? It is sweeter to trust in Jesus than not to. He will carry all your burdens."

Another woman who rose to speak had so mild a voice that what she said was only an indistinct murmur to all except those very near her. She closed what she said with a prayer.

A good deal of whispering and some low tittering was done behind me, in the rear of the room, while this woman spoke; and in part this whispering was joking comment on the speaker. One young woman near me bowed her head during the prayer on the seat-back in front of her, and a companion whispered, —

"I'll tell you when she gets through;" then added, to the girl

GETTING IN A LOAD AFTER SUPPER

on her other side in the same seat, "She's snoring," meaning the one with bowed head.

I learned that the sitters in the back of the room made their jovial inclination apparent quite often, and that sometimes certain of the more sedate and older attendants sat among them to encourage order.

A third woman said : " If we have Christ within us he helps us. Every day he is a help. In my own experience, only the other day, I had something come up that shows how he helps us. It was something that I didn't see how I could do. Then I prayed to God to help me do it just as willingly as if it was a pleasure. After that I did it without any trouble at all. When little trials come up in my daily tasks, it is a great comfort to lift up my voice in a prayer for help. Yet we must live a life of prayer, or this indwelling of Christ won't help us. The way Christ helps me is simply by the assurance that I can have his help continually if I seek it."

The man who followed this speaker said : " It costs something to be a Christian. Some point their finger at the man who becomes a Christian, and say, ' He's a hypocrite.' The world sneers at him. But we must live up against sin and the world. We must keep a straight course because he gives his daily help. If we put our trust in him, he will lead us safely and surely."

The question on the paper of the last one to speak was, " How does Christ help you to help others in their work ? " He said, " Christ helps by his spirit within us. He helps in bringing salvation to others by working on their spirit."

It was now close to quarter of nine, and the leader rose to make the final remarks. " I am very materialistic in my ideas," he said. " We've all got to earn our living. There's none of us here at this meeting that can live without work. We've all got to go at it — and it's a good thing. Work is good for us. Now, how does Christ help us in our work ? If you want to find out the value of a thing, use your imagination. Supposing the light of the sun should be suddenly quenched, what sort of a state would we be in ? Supposing the light of the world, Christ, had

never lived, how would it be with us now? When you go home
to-night what will be the first thing your eyes will see when you
get inside the door? It will probably be some convenience —

FROM THE HAYFIELD

something to make work easier, or to make life more comfortable
or pleasant. You owe that to the Babe of Bethlehem. We owe
every invention that makes our modern life so much more worth
living than the life of the ancients to the Christian religion.
What were men doing in England years ago? Till the Reforma-
tion came they were continually fighting. Christ's law means
peace. It teaches good behavior. We owe a great deal to the
Christian religion. Every one was once quarrelling, burning, kill-
ing. We would have a state of heathenism if it wasn't for the
Christian religion. We are all better for it. There have been

quite a number of testimonies to-night. You have told how Christ helps you. Christ will help you in the great battles of life. He will give his help in the little every-day trials. We need it. When we are cheerful, things go easy. When we are downcast, things go hard. Then you may think you haven't a friend in the world, but you have. It's God; it's Christ."

The meeting was then brought to a close. People fell to visiting, and the audience drifted loiteringly toward the back part of the room and out into the cold night. A scud of snow was whirling through the air. The dusky groups from the church huddled their wraps about them, bent their heads against the blast, and hurried away across the roadway or along the paths. Others bundled into the wagons brought up to the church-steps from the horse-sheds. Then the inner lights were turned out, and the church was left blank and dull and deserted.

XI

THE MINISTER

THE country preacher is a man of good education and of upright character, and he has the respect of his fellow-townsmen. He is apt in many ways not to be practical, — not to have a keen understanding of business and of life ; yet his management, or quite possibly it is that of his wife, of his home affairs is rarely otherwise than thrifty. He does not suffer from want ; and when, late in life, he retires, he may have accumulated a competence. The minister has to economize, it is true ; but in that he is very like most of his congregation. He is pretty sure to be married, and to have a family to whom he is ambitious to give a good education. After the children get through the town schools, the expense of sending them to the higher institutions of learning is considerable ; and it is in those years that the minister's coat gets most threadbare, and then it is he feels most keenly the importance of having his salary paid promptly.

The minister's children are in most instances cleverer than the average. There are cases of black sheep, but they are not common. Nearly always the minister's children are quick-witted and capable, and are not much given to sowing wild oats. After their

CUTTING RYE

education is finished, they turn to school-teaching, at least at
first ; and, whatever their final employment, they usually do well,
even financially, unless it be a case where a son follows in his
father's footsteps and becomes a minister. To become a minister
is synonymous with remaining poor in nine cases out of ten. The
ministry is not a thing to go in to for money-making. Still, I
fancy the country minister's income is up to the average of that of
his parishioners. If some of the farmers who sit under him get
more money for their work in a year than their pastor, it is because they are cleverer in their calling than he is in his. But if
the minister is bright and progressive, he does not stay in the
country. He climbs the ladder that leads to larger towns and to
more wealthy churches.

The average country minister is not a man of vigorous individuality. He is mild in speech, thought, and action. He does not
stir men up to battle; he is not very original in his thought. His
sphere is more that of the nurse ; he is rather soothing, on the
whole, even when he talks about the fiery pit, and the broad road
that leads to destruction. He may set a hearer's conscience to
pricking a little at times ; but that is less because he is particularly keen, than because the hearer's nature happens to be particularly sensitive. One can usually come away from a sermon
with his self-esteem fortified rather than humbled.

" Practical sermons," that is, sermons that touch directly the
problems of every-day life, are becoming more common ; but in
the country pulpit the theological sermon is still the rule. God,
his ways and purposes, and the plan of salvation, are dwelt on
with great detail ; and God's dealings with men, past, present,
and prospective, are all settled with remarkable certainty. The
preacher seems to understand the geography of heaven and the
mind of God much better than he understands the virtues and
shortcomings and needs of his own town. One of his greatest
pleasures is the dissecting some obscure passage of Scripture, and

showing up the true meaning of it, so that some sermons are like a bean-soup made up of one bean to four quarts of water.

I suppose a "practical" sermon has possibilities of rousing antipathy in the congregation, which the minister is inclined to avoid. He is on safe ground in theology, unless he is vigorously independent and progressive; and the country preacher is not often that. If he has heresies, they are mild ones — interesting matter for a rather colorless argument with the deacons.

Of course the preacher has his critics. He is a man whose ways and sayings are sharply watched ; and I never have known the people of a church to be united in liking their minister until they had lost him. But it is not his theology that troubles them. It is his personality, — he is too sober, or too lively; doesn't gesture enough in his sermons, or gestures too much ; visits at the house next door oftener than he does at our house ; preaches without notes and is stupid, or is stupid because he can't preach except with his written sermon before him ; and, worst of all, it may be his flock doesn't fancy his wife. At any rate, some like, and some dislike him ; and some avoid him, and some advise him ; and, take it altogether, he often has a "hard row to hoe;" while his wife, pulled about by all the fussy, opinionated, or assertive women of the church, and expected to take all the responsibilities they see fit to put upon her, is as little to be envied as her husband.

In the case of a minister who is young and unmarried, the parish feels special interest in observing whether he discovers an affiliation for any of the young women of the church ; and a girl can hardly be ordinarily considerate in her attentions to him without its being said that it is " shocking the way she runs after the minister." Every girl who is getting along in her twenties is credited with an ever-present purpose to "catch" some one; and there is supposed to be a fresh flutter of hearts among these young women every time a marriageable man moves into town. Very likely there is a fraction of truth in this view ; anyhow, the advent of a disengaged young minister, whether it makes maiden hearts pit-a-pat or not, does set tongues wagging, and keeps them wagging till he relieves the public mind by marrying.

The country pastor feels in duty bound to be social, to visit

WAITING

his people at their homes, and to be on hand at all entertainments given in connection with the church. He is, or is supposed to be, prominent on all such occasions, and is expected to be cheerful, and even jovial, however dismal he feels. But there are compensations — at the religious meetings it is entirely in keeping to be solemn to the point of mournfulness. Most ministers cultivate a sober demeanor, and there is usually an artificial setness and droop about the mouth that is due to their calling ; but they are not, as a class, so dismal as you might imagine from their sermons. When two or three of them get together, they spend a good deal more time telling each other funny stories than in talking theology.

The children of the church stand in considerable awe of the minister. He belongs to a separate world from theirs, and his pulpit manner and the matter of his sermons are pretty much outside their understanding. When the children get well along in their teens, they may really be afraid of the minister, and will systematically avoid him. If he calls at the house, they may even run to the barn and hide in the haymow, or take to the woods if the woods are handy. The fear is that he will want to talk religion to them, and want them to join the church. There is something vague and mysterious about religion and joining the church, and it makes them very uncomfortable to talk with the minister on such subjects. They know little about it, anyway, and cannot do much but to agree with what he says. They have always heard that what he says is so, and they suppose it is so ; and at the end of the halting discomfort of these talks the young person is likely to agree to join the church.

In old-time sermons, within the memory of those now living, there used to be a great deal of brimstone, and the wrath of God was found a fruitful topic to dwell on. Now sermons have a mellower tone ; and God's wrath, though not forgotten, is left as a misty background to his love. Scares are not much used except in times of revival. Then the feelings of the young people without the fold are harrowed unmercifully, and in a successful meeting there is an undertone of hysterical excitement that is very fruitful in providing future church-members.

But the usual Sabbath discourse is soothing and prosy ; and the hearers rarely show any special feeling about it, either of enthusiasm or of disagreement. Still, there is always a moral tinge to what the minister says, and in a gentle way it has its uplifting effect. Probably this and the example of the preacher's own good character count for a good deal in the long run. He might do better ; so could almost every one, no matter what the calling is.

PITCHING DOWN HAY FOR THE COWS

Unless the minister is a very young man, or newly settled, he
is elected to the school committee, very likely is chairman of it.
That necessitates his spending a day every now and then visiting
schools. The one or more schools in the home village he walks
to, but those in the outlying districts he always goes to in a team.
Our Americans are not much at walking — only tramps walk, and
they will steal or beg
a ride when they can.
The higher a man's
position, or the greater
his wealth, the less he
depends on his feet.
You may often meet
an English clergyman
walking leisurely along
the lanes and roadways
about his parish, and
he may be out on busi-
ness or only on pleas-
ure. But it is other-
wise with our New
England clergy; the
minister who walks
much must be exu-
berantly youthful or
cranky, very likely
both. When a min-
ister has really settled
in a place, and is mar-
ried, and things take

GETTING CORN FOR THE SILO

on the calm that makes it look as if there lay his life-work, he
begins to be oppressed with the vacancy of the little barn back of
the parsonage. He longs for a horse. The result is that he buys

a steady-going creature that does not cost too much ; and I think
he takes a good deal of satisfaction in the ownership, and in taking care of it. The horse is one of the sober, jogging sort —
meditative, like its master, one that keeps along somewhere near
the middle of the road, no matter where the driver's thoughts
wander. For a minister to buy a fast horse, or one that is
frisky and coltish, would seem to indicate that he himself had distinct moral lacks. Anyway, one could be quite sure that he had
mistaken his calling. Frequently a minister is not satisfied with
the possession simply of a horse, and he invests also in a cow.
With a cow and a horse in the barn, and a garden near by, and a
bit of grassland adjoining which the cow can be tethered on, the
life of the country parson is very well rounded out.

In case the clerical member of the school committee does not
own a horse, there is always a neighbor who has a creature of
proper soberness ; and this neighbor will let the horse to him for a
very modest sum — perhaps fifty cents, perhaps twenty-five cents,
for a half-day. The school committee in country places are people of fair intelligence, but rarely of special culture. Of teaching,
as a science, they know almost nothing ; and they have many of
the old-fashioned ideas that are the result of their experience in
the kind of schools they attended in their youth. Still, a com-
mitteeman is not backward about criticising. He tells the teachers how to teach, and he questions the scholars in such ways as he
calculates will bring out their wisdom or their lack of it ; and
finally makes them a little speech, in which he gives some moraliz-
ing advice, and says he "is pleased with the general appearance of
the school." The teachers feel more worried than helped by
the visits, and I would not wonder if there were teachers who had
a cry over some of these visits afterwards. There are committee
men and women who are almost brutal in what they will say and
do ; but, more usually, they are not very sharp-edged, and some of
them like to tell funny stories and crack jokes with the children.

The minister is apt to be more considerate than his farmer col-
leagues; yet his ministerial dignity is sometimes rather oppressive,
and most teachers are sure to be more thankful when he goes

FILLING THE SILO

than when he comes. The minister is very certain to get for his
school work as much as fifty dollars a year, sometimes, it may be,
as much as seventy-five or eighty dollars.

Weddings are another source of income. Probably few cou-
ples come to him who are so niggardly as to put him off with the
lawful fee of one dollar and a half. He is pretty safe for a five-
dollar bill, and may even hope for a ten. I do not think a minister
enjoys weddings, — few of those most concerned do; it is only
the sightseers and the gossips, and they find a certain enjoyment
in a funeral. But he cultivates a cheerful aspect, even if, in the
party that follows the ceremony, he is at a loss what to say, and

what to do with himself. Things might be a good deal worse, and he would still rejoice in frequent weddings for the financial gain there is in them.

Other extras come to the minister in the shape of an occasional present of choice vegetables from his farmer hearers, or a piece of meat from a recent butchering. Once in a great while, too, the people may be moved to make up a purse for him, or to have a regular surprise party of giving. I have read about the terrors of donation parties; but I think their more offensive features are now to be found mainly in the pages of humorous literature.

As a rule, the country church finds hard work in raising even the small salary it agrees to pay, and the minister has to wait for his money. This is very unpleasant; and some ministers, every now and then, when things are at a worse pass than usual, will preach a sermon on the virtues of fulfilling obligations and paying one's debts promptly.

When a minister leaves his church to go to another, he preaches a farewell sermon, in which he does some plain speaking to his people. He reviews his ministry, tells how much work he has done, number of sermons preached, funerals attended, and other details; and in an indirect way he does not fail to tell them of their shortcomings in their dealings with him, and the hard time he has had. There's no sleeping in church that Sunday. What he says stirs up, and even angers, some of the hearers. Others may be moved to tears. A man has to be undoubtedly bad or very incompetent to be let go with no regrets. He has his partisans; and there are sure to be some, especially among the women, who feel for him and look up to him.

The minister who dies in the field where he has long labored is bound to get a tribute at his funeral. The affections of the people are his, though they may never have voiced them. He has been a central figure of their life. He may never, even in his best days, have been a vital, vigorous power for uplift in the town,

but in a non-insistent, conservative way his influence has always
been on the side of kindliness and good morals. His fellow
townspeople respect his position, and they honor his life. I think
his end is often enviable, though he may have lived through many
years of hardship.

XII
A CHAPTER OF SENTIMENT

ONLY a part of the girls of a young man's acquaintance are
available; for many of them already have beaux when he
begins to look around, and only a part of the available ones will
accept his company. But from among these he picks out the one
whose looks, manner, character, and habits he finds most to his
mind. It is no very serious matter, his first fancies; he picks
out a girl for the pleasure of her present companionship, and because it is the fashion to have a girl, and he feels impelled to do
as the other fellows do. Chance and small differences often make
breaks in these companionships; and boys change girls, and girls
change beaux, and the changes seem not to matter much. But
later, when the young man's thoughts turn to marriage, he becomes
more practical. The girl he then courts is considered not only in
her personal attraction, but her family and fortune are put in the
balance for weighing also. Yet in the country it is the girl herself, usually, that attracts the man, independent of other consider-
ations. A young man very much prefers a girl whom he thinks
good-looking and good-tempered; but, if such will not have him,

A TALK WITH THE HIRED GIRL

.

he consoles himself with some one less fair and less amiable. He likes, too, that his girl should carry herself well, should have some style about her. But if he cannot get that kind, he takes up some one humbler.

The average girl is about equally particular as to whom she goes with. The going begins when she is in the midst of her teens, but it is not till two or three years later that it gets to be serious. With many of the girls the fact that they have a young man is much more important than the kind of person he is.

AUTUMN

A girl takes the fellow that happens to fall to her lot, even if he is much her inferior. She will even stick to such a person with a good deal of faithfulness. This is partly because her feelings get engaged by the romance of the companionship, or it may be simply because no one more attractive offers himself. Courtship itself is flattery. That some one picks her out and desires her company is pleasant to the girl's self-esteem, and the young man shows a willingness to serve her and do her bidding that she gets from no one else in the world. A girl is not captured primarily by character, or mental attainment, or harmony of tastes, but by the flattery of the young man's attentions. It is just as we see it among the birds. The young man bird wins his lady by the slickness and gayety of his dress, and by the sweetness of his song, and the constancy of his attentions and caresses.

The church, oddly enough, is one of love's chief highways. At a country prayer-meeting the attendants may be nearly all old people ; but at most meetings, whether religious or otherwise, indoors or out-doors, the young people are present in goodly numbers, and often make up the major part of the company. The simple fact that they are young is one reason for the going, for youth has sap and energy that age lacks. Then, they are gregarious. Boys like the company of other boys, and girls like the company of other girls ; but deeper still lies the fact that boys and girls like the company of each other. It rarely happens that young people go to a meeting from a sense of duty. Habit has something to do with it, but the impulse comes largely from the social instinct and the mutual attraction felt by the young men and the young women for each other's company. If one is to judge by their actions, their feeling is that they cannot get together too often.

The evening meetings are more relished by the young people than those of the daytime, for in the evening the young men are privileged to accompany the girls home. Sunday morning service, for instance, is less attractive, in that the family groups are kept intact, and the girls ride away with their own home people. But there is some chance for the young people to see each other, and glimpses are not impossible even in service time. Occasionally you will find a young man so well placed that he can look at the girl he most fancies all through meeting, without being made thereby conspicuous. Yet the fixedness of his gaze may often betray him, nevertheless. Other young men, who are less deeply

THE GAME OF CHECKERS

smitten by a particular one, or who are less steadfast, let their eyes roam around quite freely; and by the end of the service they are able to discourse with wisdom on the attractions, or lack of attractions, of every girl in church. Of course, there are many young men who look at the preacher all through service, but that is sometimes because they sit so near the front that there is not much else to look at. I think the girls' eyes and minds do not rove as much as the boys' do. Still, they seem to be pretty well posted about everything seeable afterwards.

XII. A CHAPTER
OF SENTIMENT

There are young men whose inclinations do not run to church-going. But, if the girl such an one fancies goes, he very likely becomes an attendant of his own accord, or he will go because the girl asks him to go. Perhaps he thus forms a habit of church-going that will stick to him. But the lazy and unprincipled, after the wife is caught, seem often to have no further use for the church, and drop once more back into their old selves.

An occasional use of a team is considered, among all but the very poor, both in city and country, an essential part of courting. The young man of humble circumstances in the city is very much handicapped in this matter. A team for a few hours costs as much as several gallons of soda-water would, and the expense makes fearful inroads on his surplus capital. In the country the young farmer has always a team at his command free of charge, and, in this respect, has great advantage over his city brother. Still, I am not certain that his courtship runs more smoothly on that account.

Probably what the young man prizes most in all his keeping company with a young lady are the visits he pays her at her home. The evenings he spends with her are very sure to number at least two, and there are those who are not content with less than twice or three times that many, and even then they throw in a few extra daytime visits. Such assiduity is held by many to be unwise, in that there is danger that the girl will get sick of the fellow who hangs around so much. I think two evenings a week is about the orthodox number; and with these, and such extra meetings as chance to come between whiles, most of the young people worry along very well.

The young man, when he makes his evening calls, is always very prompt about coming, and he shows an equal lack of promptness about going. The youth who leaves before eleven is either lukewarm in his affections, or he is remarkably considerate. On the other hand, it is the general opinion of

every one, except, possibly, of the two most concerned, that
the young man who stays after midnight is rather overdoing
the matter.

In most houses there is a parlor that is not needed evenings
for family use, and the two young people have that room to themselves. When there is a light in the parlor, the neighbors usually
know what the reason of it is. The neighbors take a good deal
of interest in the young people's love affairs. They watch their
goings and comings, and comment very freely. What they don't

IN THE PASTURE

know they guess at. They take not a little pleasure in posting
each other on new developments and imaginings, and in crack-
ing jokes on the subject. There are a good many who like to

quiz the lovers, and try their wit on them. Most of this talk is
cheap and shallow. It is not often ill-natured, but it is very apt
to descend to meddling and unkindly gossip. Perhaps there are
roses along the lovers' path, but there are thorns on the bushes.
The usual effect on those talked about is to make them callous,
and to bring them into the same habits of talk about others.

Just when two become engaged is usually uncertain, for they
often are in no haste about advertising the fact. They give the
public two or three weeks — and perhaps a year or more — to
guess about the matter. People do a vast amount of wondering
as to whether there really is an engagement or not — "They've
been goin' together long enough to be engaged, anyhow." There
is no formal way of announcing an engagement that has the
sanction of custom or fashion. The thing is simply allowed to
leak out authoritatively. Probably it had been leaking out un-
authoritatively for a long time before. There are those who
never will acknowledge to an engagement. They will even deny
it clear up to their wedding-day. Bashfulness may be the reason
for this; but usually it is the idea that this reticence is rather
clever, — it is a game, in which the public is trying to find out,
and you are trying to keep them from finding out.

Often the announcement comes when a girl begins to wear
an engagement ring. Some girls are very proud that they are
engaged and have a ring, and they take all pains to make the
new ring conspicuous. They keep the ring hand well in view
all the time, and you can send in your congratulations as soon as
you please. Whenever an engagement is announced, all the
friends are supposed to hasten to congratulate the lovers, whether
they think they have been wise or otherwise, or whether they
know anything about the matter or not. But they mostly like
to do it. I fancy the congratulations are bubbles, that, if pricked,
would collapse. They are customary, therefore we give them.
We rather enjoy the society formality of the thing; and, it being

a matter of society, we do not feel it necessary to think whether
we mean exactly what we say or not. A good deal more interest attaches to seeing how the congratulated ones will take our
words, and what they will say, than in doing the thing itself. As
for the receivers of these favors, they accept them all seriously,
and enjoy the stir they are making in the world.

When the engagement has been announced, things have been
pretty definitely settled, and
the courtship may be said to
have ended. The girl is won,
and the public is witness to
the fact. The betrothed may
quarrel and part yet ; but that
is quite improbable, — at least,
the parting is. It is not so
certain that they will not
quarrel.

For a long time before
the wedding, the girl spends
most of her time dressmak-
ing, with perhaps more or

TACKING A BEDQUILT

less practice thrown in under her mother's guidance in the art
of housekeeping. A good supply of wearing apparel, besides
the wedding-gown, on which the chief effort is expended, is
considered essential. A good many learn by experience that it
was more essential than they had any idea of when the pre-
parations were under way ; for, in the years to come, it is often
difficult to find either the time or money to provide more.

The young man, meantime, puts in a new front door at his
house (which the neighbors take as a sure sign that he is going
to be married right away), and gives his mind to getting enough
ready money together to enable him to pay the necessary expenses of the approaching wedding. If the girl has a little sum

laid aside, it is quite apt to be expended on new furniture and carpets for the house.

The wedding is pretty sure to be in the evening; and the kitchen, sitting-room, and parlor are crowded with friends. The whole premises have been furbished up; and in the parlor there are trimmings of green, and a bower has been made in a corner for the betrothed couple to stand under during the ceremony. The hour arrives, and some one plays a march on the organ, which nobody listens to, while the couple come in from where they have been waiting up-stairs. Then the solemn tones of the preacher are heard in the ceremony, and perhaps some tears are shed by the near women relatives of the couple, and many others of the guests feel as if they were at a burial; yet every one is eager to see, and all crowd into the room that can, and the un-favored ones crane their necks for a sight, and out in the hall-way one or two get on chairs and look over the others' heads. Now the "Amen" is said; and the company circulate around to shake hands with the "happy couple," and kiss the bride, and wish them happiness, and everybody cracks a joke if he can think of one. Pretty soon visiting becomes general, though it often drags, and the company breaks up into groups, and in the kitchen some of the men smoke a social cigar. There is great interest in visiting another room, where are displayed the wed-ding-presents. They get a lot of things they never in the world would buy for themselves, and very likely enough parlor lamps to stock a store.

Presently plates are passed, and cake and coffee go around; and a little later it is noticed that the bride and groom have disappeared. This is the signal for bringing out bags of rice, and setting a watch at the foot of the stairs; and some of the young men go out and find the hack or other team the couple is ex-pected to leave in, and decorate it with strips of old sheets torn up for the purpose. The young people in-doors while away the time by throwing the rice at each other ; and if a young man can slip a few kernels down a girl's neck, or fill her frizzes with them, he thinks himself very funny. Perhaps she thinks he is funny, too ; for she only plays at anger, and tries to pay him off in coin

THE VILLAGE BURYING GROUND

of the same sort. When the couple appear at the head of the stairs, the rice begins to fly thickly ; and the married pair have to run a gantlet that fairly drenches them, and that follows them clear out to the team. Not always, for they sometimes manage to escape by a back way or by a window, which makes their demonstrative friends feel rather wronged.

Usually the young couple go on a wedding-trip of a week or two, though they keep it a secret where they are going, or even as to whether they are going at all or not. Many adjourn at once to the home where they are to begin housekeeping. Sometimes they are given a tin-pan and tin-horn serenade on their arrival at their new home, but this form of rowdyism is less common than it has been.

Probably after marriage a good deal of the romance of the courtship fades into commonplace. There usually grows with years a warm undertone of affection for the home and its various members, but it is in New England life very undemonstrative. Caress and attentive courtesy and words of love are absent; nor is the man at all particular, as he was in the days of courtship, to be neat in his dress or habits. If he is slovenly and dirty, and odorous of sweat and stale tobacco, the old-time charm can hardly continue. Nor is the woman the same as before. She may be of flighty temper, or ailing, or untidy, and a poor house-keeper ; and now, in a house of her own, these qualities come out.

Nevertheless, if the love on both sides has been genuine, something of the old feeling is pretty sure to cling, and there grows a quiet fondness for each other that only death will break. Neither would I mention death, if it were not that widows and widowers show such an aptness for finding consolation in new partners. They do not care to live on memories. When a man loses his wife, he is not expected to waste many months in look-ing up some available woman willing to fill the double place of second wife and housekeeper. As to the widows, they seem to be " willin'." In New England, just the same as elsewhere, the prose and poetry of life are pretty well mixed ; and you can find whatever you look for, — comedy, tragedy, the heroic, the mean, and a great deal that is simply aimless and colorless.

XIII

DESERTED HOMES

EMIGRATION among the would-be tillers of the soil began early from the New England coast to the fertile meadows along the inland rivers. When the more productive of these lowlands had been taken, the settlers began to push back among the hills, whose rugged, tumbled masses cover so much of New England's little corner of the United States. To those familiar with the vast tracts of our country so greatly superior in fertility and accessibility, this hill region seems to hold for the farmers very little attraction. But at the time it was settled, little was known of the West. By contrast with the sandy plains along the coast it was very rich, and the crops sent down from the hill farms were considered something wonderful.

The land amongst the hills could be had almost for the asking. The emigrants to them were not mere adventurers, seeking gold or sudden wealth ; they sought homes, and they did not hope to possess these homes except by hard labor and strict economy. Such pioneers are men of energy and thrift, and are bound to win prosperity, even though circumstances seem adverse.

Each family was in those times a little world in itself. The farm furnished not only food and clothing, but the very house for the family shelter. Woodland was all about, and there were many little sawmills along the streams where the trees could be converted into beams and boards. The farmer himself did much of the work preparatory to the building, and all the neighbors lent ready assistance at the raising.

Every farm had its field of flax and its flock of sheep. These furnished the raw material for clothing, which the women of the family spun into thread, wove into cloth, and made into garments. Farming and household utensils and much of the furniture were home-made. A maple orchard furnished most of the sugar used. Wants which the family was dependent on the outside world to supply were simple and few. Needed supplies from without they readily obtained by exchange of products at the village store ; and an occasional wagon-load of farm-produce carried to one of the large towns, or the surplus of their herds and flocks driven thither, brought them wealth. A comfortable home was the near, clear object on which the young people set their eyes ; and they expected to win it by sturdy work in the manner to which they were used.

The family and home town bounded the world then. What lay beyond was but vaguely known. Now wider and fuller knowledge makes self and a quiet village life seem contracted. The newspaper and literature give wide outlooks to the humblest home, from one end of the globe to the other. In the reader's ears, however remote his habitation, is a continual hum of strange sounds, — the waves of the sea, the din of crowded city streets, the thud of the pick as the miner searches for treasure in the far West, the clicking of the reapers in the wide grain-fields of the prairies, and the ring of gold and silver money as it changes hands in the world's trade and commerce. The dweller in the weatherworn little house among the secluded New England hills hears all this ; and as he follows the slow plough across the rocky

IN A SHEEP PASTURE

fields, or swings the scythe beneath the hot skies of summer, is it any wonder he sees visions of fortune or fame beckoning him ? At the very best there will be whispers in the breezes of quicker gains for lighter labor, and of enlivening sights and sounds to be gained by a change of abode.   All this makes the bond of seclusion chafe, and many go and few return.

Had the Puritans gone up the Mississippi, and settled on the rich lowlands of the Middle States, New England would still be largely given up to forests.   The land West gives so much larger returns for the same expenditure of time and labor in the case of most crops, that our rocky uplands would naturally have been

A PICNIC

the last to be utilized.   Still, the advantage of the West over the East was not marked till the railroads made transportation easy, and farm machinery was invented to do the work which had been done by hand and required many laborers. These machines could be used to advantage only in large and level fields. Such fields the West had, and our hills had not. New England could no longer compete with the West, which now had fertile soil, clear, broad fields, railroads, and labor-saving machinery all in her favor. The scythe was antiquated, yet much of the hill grass-land could only be mown by hand. Planting, cultivating, reap-ing, and threshing were in the West all reduced to a science. In the East nature compelled the slow old methods. Besides, in all old communities there is the tendency to follow very closely the ways which have become habitual. As their fathers worked, so the new generation works; but a living no longer can be made in the old ways. Success is only with the few who can adapt themselves to the changing times and their needs.

As a rule, it was the most energetic who emigrated to the more promising fields of the West. This left behind those who were least fitted to cope with altered conditions and increased competition. Life and living have become more complicated. The farm no longer furnishes all the necessaries of life as it did formerly. Food, clothing, house furnishings, and farm tools have to be bought to a much larger extent than before. Carpets and wall-paper call for a periodical outlay. A set of upholstered furniture for the parlor is aspired to, and the girls of the family feel that their happiness depends on their having a melodeon.

Travelling has grown more general with the increase of rail-roads; and journeying, which in stage-coach days held small at-traction, is now considered a necessity. It has become a great trial to live far removed from a railroad station. " Every one nowadays wants to go somewhere once in a while." The pos-session of railroads, and hence facilities for travel, gives to all the large places a magnetic power over the dwellers in the outlying towns. More important still as an element of city attraction is the thought among the young people that their home village is dull and slow. They long to get where there is more life and movement. It has become the rule for boys to leave for the cities somewhere between the ages of fifteen and twenty ; and

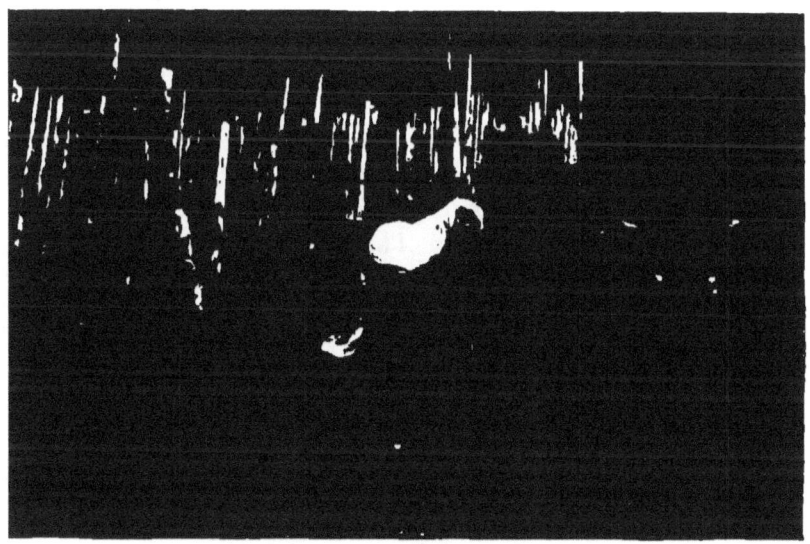

LOOKING AT HIS CUCUMBERS

each lad, as he grows up, naturally follows the example of his older brothers and the other village boys. "The young people don't like the country," you are told. "If you don't let 'em go of their own accord they'll run away before they'll stay." It may be in time that the parents, too, leave the old homestead, and go to live with one of their children, or they wait until death calls them, and another is added to the lonely, deserted houses amongst the hills. The children have no use for the old place, and it is sold for whatever it will bring at auction. Probably it is not at once given over to decay. There are in all communities certain people of a roving disposition who own no homes, but rent a house

as convenience dictates. They take some place where rents are
low, and there abide until the fever of unrest calls them to move
on again. The homes which the old families have left are usually occupied for a number of years by a succession of these
rovers. Such tenants are apt to be shiftless in their tendencies ;
and the place gets out of repair, and the out-buildings sag and
lean, and fall to pieces. When the house has seen its last occu-
pant, it is usually convenient to make it a storage-place for apples,
farm-tools, and odds and ends ; but it receives slight care, and
decay makes swift havoc. Even the little mendings which the
most shiftless would make for their own comfort if the house
was their home are neglected. The roof gets leaky, the window-
panes fall in or get broken, a door loses its hinges, a stone in
the underpinning is displaced ; and these little beginnings are not
long in making the dwelling a broken mass of fallen bricks and
timbers. Each year the scanty grass of the farm fields is har-
vested, and the apples picked ; but the land is not helped by
fertilizing, and bushes start up all along the walls, and encroach
on the open fields, and Nature seems in a fair way to take the
whole place back to herself once more.

For the last forty years or over this process has been going
on, and the farm population of New England has been decreas-
ing. Even the valley towns in close proximity to railroads and
city markets show a depletion, and unoccupied houses can be
found along the finest of our old village streets. But their numbers increase with the distance from railroads and markets, and
many of the remote towns have lost nearly half their inhabitants.
Usually the vacant houses are scattered about singly, but there
are places in the outlying districts where you may come on whole
groups of them.

Most of these deserted houses that one sees along our country ways are low, brown little buildings which have never been
painted, or which have been so long strangers to a paint-brush

that the old tints have almost disappeared. A reddish tone lingers on the loosening clapboards of some, showing them to date back to the early years of the century, when red was considered the most pleasing color for a dwelling. Yet once in a while you will find houses of more recent date, roomy and substantial and comfortable. The majority of these, however, need considerable repairing inside and out to make them pleasantly habitable ; and many are partly fallen in, or so decayed that repairs are out of the question.

The reasons for desertion do not vary much, and if you look

COWS IN THE BARNYARD

for a romance or a tragedy connected with these forsaken homes you in most cases look in vain. It is but a prosy story the neighbors tell. "Two old people lived there all alone," they say of the house you inquire about. "A year ago the woman died,

and now two months ago the man died. No one wants to move
into our town nowadays ; so the farm's sold to one of the neighbors for little or nothing, and there the house is all shut up."

"The family that lived over in the house you're talkin' about
never amounted to much here ; and they've gone down to Factory Village, and the whole family of 'em's workin' in the mills
there."

"How do they get along there?"

"Well, I don't know. They was always kind o' shiftless.
They take in considerable money, but they don't save nothin'."

The story of another runs in this wise.

"The last time that little house above here was occupied
there was just one old woman lived there all alone. All her
relations was dead, or had forgotten her, or didn't care nothing about her ; and the town had to support her mostly. She
had a little garden, and the neighbors helped her some ; but
two years ago one of the women here called, and found her
dead. It ain't much of a place, anyway. 'Tain't likely anybody'll want to live there again."

One grief of the young people on the farm is the lack of
ready money. To have spending-money and smart clothes is to
a boy apt to be one of the heights of his ambition. In the
country the attainment of these things is wofully hard. If you
work for your father on the home farm, he does not pay wages ;
and there is difficulty in making him see your need of pocket-
money as you see it yourself. In the majority of cases, even if
the father were willing to supply the boy's calls, he can spare
little money for anything beyond absolute necessities. In earlier
times there was no alternative but to work on where one was,
and there were few things one needed to buy. But when the
factories began to spring up, there was call for laborers, and the
way at once opened to earning ready money. This first set
the current of life in the country flowing into the cities. The

reason for the current continues to exist, and so does the direction of the flow.

It is the attraction of the city which is at present the chief cause of the depopulation of the New England country. The

A FEED FOR THE SHEEP

new lands of the West have largely been taken up, and emigration has ceased in that direction. The West has the advantage in raising wheat, corn, and other great crops; but many localities in the East are especially favored for dairy-farming and market-gardening. The people do not leave the farms because a living cannot be made. This is the case at times, but is not the rule. The impossibility of making a living is often asserted, and has wide acceptance; but it would be hard to find an instance where the same thought, energy, and hard work have been used which wins success in the other callings which does not win success as well in farming. Instance after instance can be found where young men have taken farms, and, by studying the needs of the markets, and keeping their land under high cultivation, have had handsome returns. It requires hard work, and it requires system. They get their crops started early, and they try to be first with them in the markets. They pride themselves in making a reputation for always having the best of everything. Such farmers find a steady market. They win the confidence of the wealthy city residents, and get the highest prices. At the farm, the buildings are kept painted and in good repair, the stock is well housed, the fields are fertilized and made to give rich returns, and an air of busy thrift is everywhere apparent. The grounds around the house are neatly kept, and a lawn-mower is brought into frequent use to keep the grass down. In-doors is attractiveness too. The ideal farmer is not simply the man who grubs in the dirt, and his thought is not bounded by the acres he tills. He has his library ; papers and magazines are frequent visitors, and there is a piano in the sitting-room. In his thrift and success he finds satisfaction. There is a systematic strife after attainment which gives a healthful interest to his work ; and for such as he the city has slight attraction.

Of the unsuccessful class, there are always some who are burdened by circumstances beyond their control. There is a large number, however, who are burdened by their own habits and lack of thought. The man whose crops are a little late, and apt to fall short of the best quality, does not get high prices. He has a seedy, slouchy look when he comes into town with his produce. The butter, eggs, and other things he carries are put up in all sorts of old boxes, baskets, and bags ; and they lack attractiveness. Such management is not good business, and the man cannot make farming a success. He says farming does not pay. He thinks the city a sphere more suited to his talents. In time he deserts the farm, and perhaps in some factory or city shop makes very good pay. He did not put brains into his farming. Now an overseer furnishes brains, and his chief contribution is labor. In that he makes a better living than formerly, he thinks that he has demonstrated that farming did not pay; but often he has only proved that he accomplishes more under another's overseeing than under his own.

Interest in the deserted homes and in the reasons for them, and the remedy, has been widespread. Within the last few

A DESERTED HOME

years the States in which they are most numerous have undertaken to find tenants. The methods have been much the same, and an explanation of the plan adopted in Massachusetts will serve for all.

The Board of Agriculture has charge of the work. The first move was to send circulars to the assessors of each town in the State, asking them to give lists and descriptions of " abandoned or partially abandoned farms " in their vicinity. An " abandoned or partially abandoned farm " was defined to be one which was not occupied for purposes of cultivation or a summer home, and which was for sale at a low price.

Farms that had been so long abandoned that the buildings had disappeared and the land mostly grown up to brush and wood were not to be considered. Tracts of land suitable for purposes of cultivation or for grazing, even without buildings, were, however, listed. It was also noted that it would be useless to call attention to any farms but those offered for a low price in proportion to their productive capacity.

One hundred and thirty-five towns responded with reports of deserted homes. A circular was then despatched to the owner of each farm, asking for a detailed description of the farm, its buildings, its distance from post-office and railroad station, and its price. On receipt of these answers a pamphlet was prepared containing the full description of each farm, with a map and prefatory matter of general explanation. Copies were distributed free on application to the Board of Agriculture.

Most of the farms thus advertised were in hilly and broken central sections of the State, or in the western part, among the rugged regions of the Green Mountain ranges. Special stress was laid on the fact that the scenery in many of these deserted localities was of unsurpassed beauty, and that the location and surroundings of many of the farms catalogued made them ideal places for summer residences. Figures were given in the pamphlet to show that the staples of old-fashioned farming are being replaced by a different class of crops. The time when great numbers of cattle were fattened in the Connecticut valley and on the Berkshire hills, and then driven to Boston market, is past.

The wheat crop has been steadily falling off for the past fifty years. But a vast increase in the production of butter and milk shows dairy-farming to be prosperous and profitable; and figures of the same sort prove that there is gain in the raising of vegetables, poultry, small fruits, and other things. It is noted, too, that the Massachusetts farmers have one marked advantage over those in most other States. This lies in the numerous big towns and cities, which afford a good home market for what the farms produce. The business of supplying these centres of population with milk, butter, eggs, fresh fruit, and fine vegetables belongs to the farmers of the home State.

The average size of abandoned farms was found to be eighty-six acres. Their value with buildings averaged $894. Those without buildings averaged $561. The average cost of the land itself, per acre, was thus less than six dollars.

The quotation of one or two descriptions from the catalogue of farms for sale will give an idea of them all, and of the places they advertise. The following is one from among the low-priced places : —

Shutesbury. — Farm of sixty acres ; mowing, eight ; pasture, eighteen ; woodland, thirty-four ; suitable for cultivation, twelve. Almost all the grass can be cut with a machine. One-story house, five rooms, in need of some repair. Good well at house, and running water back of barn. Twenty apple and twelve other fruit trees. Railroad station, Leverett, six miles ; post-office, Shutesbury, one mile. Price, $400 ; cash at sale, $100; interest on balance, four per cent.

For an example of the more expensive farms we note this one in Windsor : Farm of one hundred and sixty four acres ; mowing, sixty ; pasture, forty ; woodland, forty-six ; suitable for cultivation, twenty. Grass can be cut with a machine. Sugar-bush, one hundred and fifty trees. House seven rooms ; fair repair. Brook in pasture ; two wells, one in cellar, one in barn. Seventy-

five apple-trees. Railroad station, Dalton, four miles ; post-office,
Windsor, two miles. Price, $1,200 ; cash at sale, $600 ; interest
on balance, six per cent. School, half a mile ; church and cheese-
factory, two miles.

This effort of the State led to a great deal of discussion in the
newspapers, and there were numerous applications for the cata-
logues. Most interest was awakened in the well-to-do residents
of the large towns. Their object was to procure for themselves,
at a moderate price, a country home for the summer. For all-the-
year-round homes, as farms pure and simple, these outlying districts seemed to lack attraction.

Some responses came from dwellers in the city who had
lost their health, and hoped by an out-door life to win back
their strength and vigor. Some wrote who in their factory work
had had the half-spoken wish for years to leave the din and
dust, and live in country quiet. But there is among such as
these great hesitancy about making the change. To leave good
wages and a safe situation for uncertainty is not easy. To many
country life is dreamed of as one of the hopes of the future
half their lives ; but they never catch more than vacation glimpses
of it, and the hope is never realized. From the West came
other inquiring letters. People who had moved from the East
had not forgotten their old homes, and were homesick.

But that the hilltowns should regain all their former prosperity does not, at present, seem probable. The winters in
particular are a great trial. With their cold and the blocked
roads they make the women of the family prisoners for months.
It requires not a little hardihood to get about in snow-time.
An old gentleman who had lived all his life among the hills, re-
marking on this, said, " The summer visitor comes up here, and
says, ' This is a glorious region,' and talks as if there was no
finer place on earth to live in. But he has just run away from
the heat and noise of the city. He'd sing a different tune if

he came up here in winter. He'd be as rabid to get away as he was to come."

In the villages there is always some little stir and society; but on the scattered, outlying farms time is apt to drag heavily. The almost inevitable result of this six months of winter lone-

PICKING APPLES

liness is that the people's lives get a touch of hopelessness. This melancholy can often be detected in the settled tone of the voice, which has become sad and complaining, even when speaking of the most ordinary and even cheerful facts.

Another burden of the hill-town farmers is the taxes. In many places they run up to twenty dollars on the thousand, and have been known to go as high as twenty-eight. It is no small task, in the majority of families, to raise the money to pay such rates. They are driven to seek a home elsewhere, in regions where the burdens are less heavy. As for would-be purchasers from the outside, whether they be poor or wealthy, they will hesitate long before buying where the yearly cost of owning property is so high.

To a man with a family who settles in a new place, the character of the schools and their accessibility become important. The hilltowns, as compared with others, are in most cases at a disadvantage. A district school education is all they usually have to offer. The school year is short ; and the teachers poorly paid, and themselves are usually graduates of no other than this same district school. They, very likely, have no further interest in the teaching than to gain a little money to help pay the home taxes, or the interest on the home debt, or more probably for their own personal expenditure. The schoolhouses are few and far between. They are lonesome little buildings, placed in some spot conveniently central for the district, many times entirely out of sight of any houses, and again in some little clearing all closed in by 'the sombre woods. The furnishing is very rude, and modern helps for study are noticeable by their absence. Some of the scholars have to travel a distance of two or three miles along the lonely, half-wooded roads to get to school, and the scholar who is not obliged to bring his dinner is an exception. The coming of settlers from the outside is not encouraged by these facts ; for no man with a family in these days of education will voluntarily place his children beyond its reach. The value of schooling is far too well understood, and its necessity for a successful battle with life is keenly felt. The prospect of good schools is now one of the potent attractions to the emigrant, and where these are lacking he will not go.

The future rural life in New England will be somewhat differ-

A SUMMER EVENING

ent from that of the past or that of the present. Along the
streams is a chance for a limited number of mills to do profitable
work, and there are many favorable opportunities for gain in
dairy-farming which need not entail seclusion or great drudgery.
The old-fashioned churning and home butter-making are things
of the past on the large farms and among the more enterprising
farmers. Instead, the cream is collected each day at the farmhouses by a man who makes that his business, and is carried to
some central point where there is a creamery. Here is a special
building where all the cream of the district is made into butter
by men who spend their whole time at it. This makes science of
the work, and some of the dairy-farms carried on in this way are
very remunerative. Farming in New England never returns a
large fortune; but it may give a comfortable home, and a snug
sum laid away in the savings-bank.

In summer the hills have their fairest aspect, and many pil-
grims from the cities resort thither to spend their vacations.
Here quiet broods, and the air is sparkling and pure. Narrow
roadways crisscross the country invitingly everywhere. They
pass through shadowy woods, across farmland clearings, along
the narrow valleys where the little streams pursue a fretting
course among the bowlders, and again high up among the sunlit,
stone-fenced pastures. Some towns, especially favored by fashion,
chance, or nature, are being quite rejuvenated by the summer
people. These outsiders often take an interest in the homes,
schools, churches, and library of the place, which results in a
substantial gain for the town in appearance, education, and refinement. By this annual inflow from the cities, the country districts are in some measure getting back what they yield to the
cities; and in this lies suggestion of a more hopeful time coming.
But if the future leaves the lonely little farms, far from neighbors, on the by-roads and some of the more barren and weather-
beaten hilltops, entirely deserted, it will be no wonder. Nor is

such a view wholly cheerless. As long as land is plenty in more favored districts, where the soil is richer, and society and modern facilities of travel more within reach, it will not make life less full if these lonely hills are again possessed by the old-time forests.

XIV

THE FARM DAY BY DAY

MOST city men of culture and refinement at times feel a strong longing for the country. The New Yorker looks out from his office window on the hurly-burly of the street with the desire to escape its unending rattle and movement. "A little hillside farm and quiet" seem to him Arcadia. Yet those who dream of farm life in their city offices seem always to have lurking doubts as to the possibility of realizing their ideal. They never become farmers. They have the fear, I suppose, it would not be all poetry when they got down to details; and there is an unpleasant vision in the mind of "getting up at four o'clock in the morning to milk eleven cows before breakfast."

The truth is, he is a lucky man among New England farmers who has cows to the number of eleven. The majority are obliged to content themselves with from one to four or five. The large farms may keep a dozen, and an occasional milk-farm may number its herd by the scores, but the average farmer keeps well within the units.

As to the four-o'clock-in-the-morning bugbear; such unearthly hours may have been kept by the forefathers, but civilization has advanced a stage in the last generation, and few farmers can be found who are in the habit of poking about among the gray morning glooms as early as four o'clock. In summer New England people rise between five and six ; in winter they rise between six and seven.

Exceptions to this rule are to be found in the milkmen and market-gardeners who supply the cities and large towns. The former are up in the neighborhood of three o'clock every morning in the year from January to December. The milk must be delivered early ; and the milkman has not only to feed and milk his cows before he starts, but often has to drive many miles to reach his market. The purveyors of vegetables and small fruits are some of them even earlier than the milkmen ; and in the season, if you live on the line of their route to the city, you may hear the slow rumble of their heavily laden wagons very soon after midnight.

Then, too, most farmers make up occasional loads of produce for the market ; and many have a set day each week on which they go to the nearest large town to supply regular customers with butter, eggs, and other farm wares Some laggards may not get started on their trips till the middle of the forenoon, but the thrifty farmer is up getting his work done and loading his wagon long before daylight. Sunrise sees him jogging along cityward. If the distance to market is not over seven or eight miles, he will get back early in the afternoon, and have time to do considerable work before supper-time.

There is always a flutter of excitement about the house when, on his return, the team turns in at the home gate. The family is always glad to see him safe back again ; and then there is the interesting problem of whether he has done the various errands the different ones intrusted to him, and whether he has done them right.

" Here comes pa," says Mrs. Farmer, as she looks out of the

TOPPING ONIONS

window. "I do hope he thought to get the yeastcake I forgot
to tell him we wanted."

She goes to the door, and all the rest of the family that
happen to be in the house at the time go with her. Mr. Farmer
calls out "Hullo!" as he alights, and begins to unhitch.

"Did you get my bunnit at the milliner's?" asks the eldest
girl.

"Yes," is the reply; "but it's under the seat, and you can't
get it till I heave off some of them things on behind there. I'll
get it when I get the horse unhitched."

The girl, to expedite matters, helps undo the harness, and
get the horse out of the shafts. Questions fly thickly; and interest is rife down to the smallest member of the household, who
hopes he, too, has been remembered with a toy perhaps, or, at the
very least, with a stick of striped candy.

Occasionally Mrs. Farmer accompanies her husband to market,
or one of the children goes with him. The younger ones have
usually pleasure for their object; the older ones, when they go,
have serious interests in the shopping-line, which they are afraid
to trust to the head of the household.

Bedtime comes early. The milkman begins to nod directly
after supper, and very probably falls asleep over the paper he is
reading. In fact, he and the market-gardener can hardly sit in
quiet ten minutes at any hour of the day without dropping off
into a nap. There is enough of muscular labor in the life of
most farm families to make them, when evening arrives, not
much inclined to mental activity. Unless visitors come in, evening is not a time of much conversation, and reading for any
length of time is pretty sure to end in dozing.

When sleepiness begins to be overpowering, that is felt to be
a sign it is time to retire, whatever the hour; and the milkman,
and the farmer who has to make an early start, disappear between
seven and eight o'clock. The others follow as the inclination

takes them. About nine o'clock, in most farmhouses, the last light has disappeared, and darkness has full sway.

New England life has several distinct environments, each in itself a study. First, there is the village life of one of the valley towns ; second, there is the life of such a town's outlying hamlets, each of which has for its public centre a little wooden schoolhouse at the meeting of the roads ; third, there is the life in the hill-town villages. Hill towns are those in the more tumbled and rugged regions of New England. At times the chief village of such a town is in the valley of some little river, but oftenest it is on the rolling sweep of a great hill. These villages, too, have their tributary hamlets, and their townships are dotted with numerous isolated farms ; and each of these environments has its distinctive effect on character, and on the attractiveness or lack of attractiveness of the homes.

The valley towns have the most thrifty look, and they have a mellow aspect that can only be given by age and a rich soil. They are characterized by beautiful lines of elms, which arch the streets, and embower the fine old mansions built seventy-five or one hundred years ago. It has become the common habit of the people to look after the neatness of their own premises, and to take an interest and pride in the general neatness of the whole village. The buildings, as a rule, are kept in good repair, and when a house approaches the borders of rustiness it receives a coat of fresh paint.

Churches and public buildings are well cared for. Indeed, the appearance of a subscription-paper which circulates with the object of raising money to modernize or beautify the sanctuary is perennial. The horsesheds in the rear of the church do not, however, receive a due share of public attention. They exist in a state of perpetual grayness and decrepitude. Yet they are not altogether neglected ; for they do receive an occasional decoration of circus posters and patent-medicine handbills, which, if it does not add to their æsthetic beauty, makes them more interesting and attractive to the children of the neighboring schoolhouse. I suppose I ought to mention in this connection that some of the big "bad boys" of that school yonder have used these same sheds on their noonings to play cards in — yes, and to learn to smoke in.

On the whole, these villages, with their two churches, their town hall and high-school building, and the two or three little stores, and numerous well-kept farmhouses, impress one very pleasantly. Farmers rarely attain to affluence ; yet there is a goodly proportion

ONE OF THE OLD VALLEY TOWNS

of them who attain to comfort, and are exemplars of a well-to-do thrift. On the other hand, many are burdened with mortgages that make life an unending struggle to win money enough to pay interest and taxes after providing for other expenses. There are many families who, in a humble way, live tragedies without themselves realizing it. Those who do realize it, and chafe under it, make the tragedy more distressing still. In reality, whether in debt or not, a chronic lack of ready money is a characteristic of a large part of the country dwellers. I fancy the selectmen of a rural town would expect to see most of the community go into bankruptcy if they insisted on having the taxes paid as soon as the bills were presented. If they can get them on the instalment plan, within six or eight months of that time, they are thankful. Yet if a family is not altogether shiftless, its troubles stop short of real suffering and total wreck. One does not need in the country more than a roof over one's head, and a garden-patch, and a flock of hens, to be sure of the bare necessaries of life. A lingering sickness, which causes continued expense, or that disables one of the workers of the family, is of all things the one to be most dreaded. The family which all along has been living on the outer edge of comfort sees hard times then. Such a casualty makes "scrimping" necessary, even among the well-circumstanced ; and, with the poor, the added care, and the weary, lengthened hours of work needed to make ends meet, is a heavy load.

The centres of the social life of a town are the church, the post-office and stores, and the hotel. There is much visiting between neighbors ; and if the question is asked what they talk about on these visits, I am afraid the answer would be, "about the rest of the neighbors." In itself the subject is not a bad one ; but the treatment is apt to be one of gossipy curiosity, and of opinion-giving that lacks largely the saving virtue of charity. Like the child who pulls the clock to pieces and then cannot put it together again, they tear down and do not build up. In good-sized villages there is a division of families into a number of sets or cliques, each with a particular buzz of

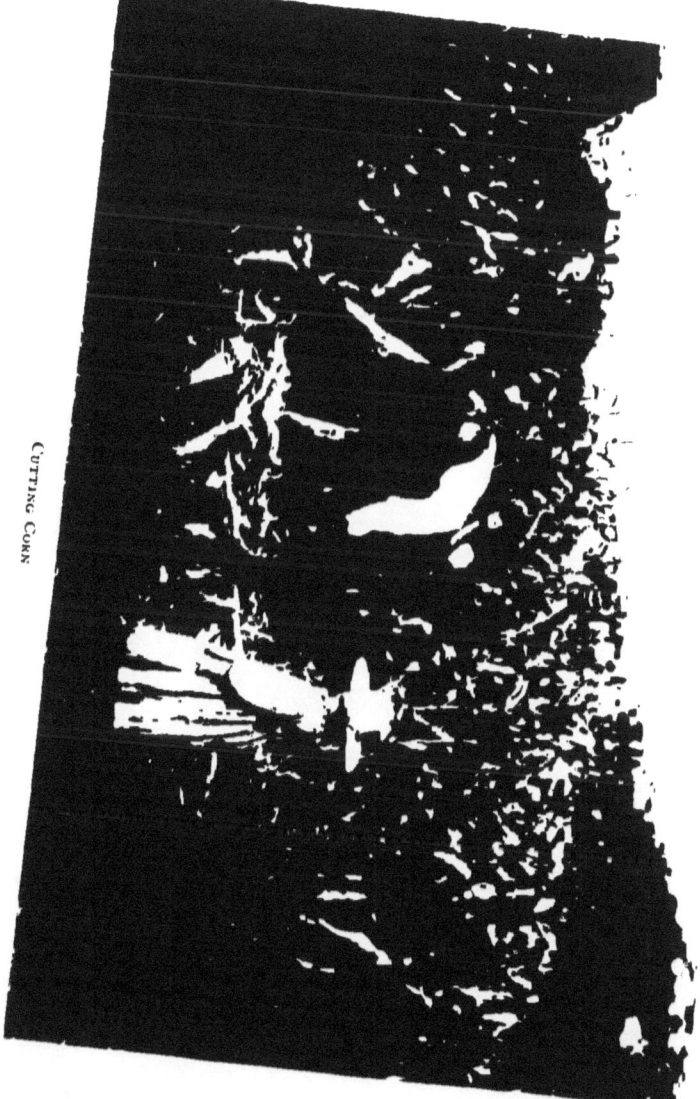

CUTTING CORN

opinion and criticism of other people's doings.   One of the best places to go to hear the news is church.   If a girl, for instance, chooses to stand around afterwards, and chatter with the others, she will get filled up with all the petty news of the neighbor-

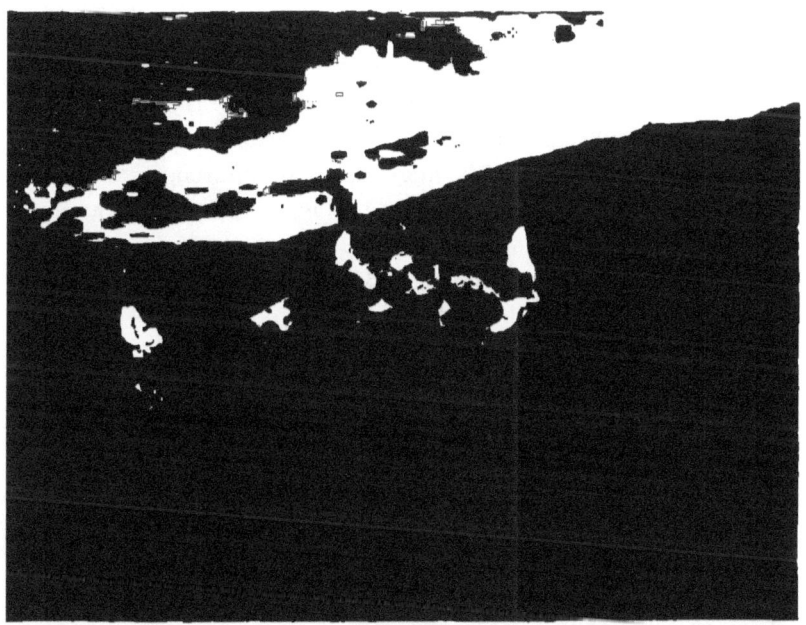

THE GEESE

hood.   Then when she comes home she has all this gossip to retail out, — what those who live around have said; all about this fellow and that girl, this beau and that, what he ought to 'a' done, and what she ought to 'a' done.   Often the girl and some of her listeners will spend a good part of an hour disputing over something that doesn't matter either way.   A funeral is always the occasion, too, of a good deal of talk.   There's hardly a detail overlooked, and even in the carriage on the way

to the grave comments are freely made on the appearance of
the fellow-mourners. " There's Bill Watson, he thinks he's made
now ! " That is the style of remark. If some minister should
preach a sermon on gossip, — and it seems to me that is a subject they incline to treat tenderly or avoid altogether, — the folks
would go home and say, " Well, such and such a one got a good
dose that time ; hope they'll think of it next time they go to
say anything against us." In many villages the worst centre of
gossip is the church sewing-society. The gossip there is at times
not only decidedly unchristian, but borders close on scandal.

In towns where there is more than one church, — and, while
most farming towns need but one, they usually have at least
two, — there is pretty sure to be a feud of more or less intensity
between the different societies. But the gossip and the feuds,
though they sometimes burst into fierce flaming and stir the whole
community, only smoulder ordinarily. Nor are the townspeople
at bottom other than amiable and well-meaning, but there is
great need that they should make kindliness more characteristic
of their social relations with their fellow-mortals.

Magazine and literary clubs have won a place in many neigh-
borhoods. Some of the literary meetings are bright and fresh-
ening, others drag, and hardly rise above the level of stupidity ;
but they all help to raise the plane of thought. Find a village
where they have had for a series of years a successful literary
club, and you will find the people decidedly superior in culture
and refinement to those of communities which have had no
club.

The church is a subject of solicitous care for quite a group
of its more actively disposed members ; for it is no easy matter
to keep the minister in bread and butter, and attend to the appeals of all the missions that look to them for help. Then, there
are the young who must be amused by special suppers and so-
ciables ; and every few years there comes the grand occasion of

a revival in the church, when attendance is imperative every evening; or there is an installation ; or there is a combined gathering of all the missionary societies of a particular kind in the county in that church. All this means a good deal of work and activity; and a large share of it means only that, to tell the truth.

As to the store, post-office, and hotel, the habit of loafing in them is easily formed. It begins with loitering there when on errands. Evenings and stormy days a good many country dwellers find time hanging heavy on their hands. On such days a group is found in each of the public resorts of the place ; and, as the fashion is, they smoke and chew and spit, and keep up an intermittent conversation of combined news, opinion, and chaff, with a mingling of profanity, and of stories of a sort much better untold. It seems astonishing that such a reeking, filthy crowd should be tolerated in respectable towns, and at the post-office, too, where the

TRAINING THE DOG

children and women have to go as well as the men.

The hotel, of all these resorts, has the most dubious reputation as a lounging-place; for it is there that liquors are sold, if the town has voted license, and a good many times when it has not voted license. The traveller through New England, who stops at its taverns need not be surprised if, after breakfast, the landlord inquires in a confidential tone if he wouldn't "like to take a little something." Or let him take a seat by the stove in the barroom through a rainy day, and note the mysterious visits to a back room of the landlord and this one or that one who has dropped in. There is an odor of whiskey on the air when they return, and yet this is a no-license town! As a rule, whatever the town votes, a hotel keeps liquors on hand for the accommodation of travellers ; and most landlords will sell on the sly to any one they know, and can trust to keep quiet about it.

The outlying hamlets of a valley town participate in part in the life of the central village, but they have their own summer picnics and Christmas-tree in the schoolhouse and their own literary circle. Often they have their own particular loafing-place for those whose taste runs in that direction. This may be a little store, or a grist-mill, or a ferryhouse on the river-bank. These hamlets and the scattered farms miss something of the activity of the larger villages ; but they miss a good deal of pettiness as well, and the boys and girls are comparatively free from the idle rowdyism of a certain class of young fellows which is an element of the life of most towns. Those children who grow up in the comparative isolation of the smaller villages and more lonely, separate farmhouses often make the most effective men and women. If they are naturally endowed with a fair share of vitality and mental vigor, the fact that they are thrown on their own resources brings out and develops capability which the more favored situations would have failed to do.

The New England country is being invaded to a considerable extent, in some places, by late emigrants from across the water. They are viewed with more or less feeling of antipathy, due to differences in habits and religion, and to the newcomer's superior thrift. The foreigner has no pride of family or of position to uphold. He adapts himself to conditions, and gets right down to hard work. Many of the Yankee families are shiftless and wasteful, and are too aristocratic on slender means to get on in the world. Besides, it is often the case that the foreigner has more physical vitality than the older settlers. With the acquisition of property and his thrifty use of it, and the education of his children at the schools, this foreign element becomes an addition of real value to the country town. At any rate, the example the newcomer sets of industrious economy is one of which there is need.

In the Dooryard

The foreigners settle almost wholly in the valley towns. Few are to be found among the hills. These continue to be the sole homes of the "double dyed and twisted Yankees." For many years the hill towns have been dwindling in size, and their life has lost much of its old-time vitality. Among the hills, the farther from the centre of trade you get, the more marked is the rugged rusticity of the inhabitants. You find some very queer ones; but the people are by no means, as a class, like those shown on the stage or in the pictures of the funny papers. Neither is there wanting ability and culture, and of originality of thought and expression there is a great deal.

On the hills are many pleasant villages and numerous thrifty farms. There are also, it must be acknowledged, on the scant-treed and thin-grassed hilltops, many villages that approach forlorn-ness; and everywhere through this country are the scattered homes which by their shabbiness make it plain that the struggle for existence is either not vigorously battled, or is against too great odds. Most of the inhabitants live without bodily discomfort; though close economy is required among the poorer families the year through, and luxuries, and very many of the ordinary refine-ments and pleasures of life, are entirely absent. Their food is almost wholly produced on the farm itself; but in an intelligent household this does not mean aught that is unwholesome, or any stinting in quantity. A meat-cart makes weekly visits in the summer to such families as can afford to patronize it, but in win-ter does not get far out of the villages. Pigs are raised on every farm, and on most a beef creature is occasionally killed. While cold weather lasts, the meat not needed for immediate use can be packed away in snow, and kept fresh till spring sets in. During the summer months the farm-folk depend on the pickled hams and salt pork they have laid away, and the beef they have corned or dried, and an occasional salt codfish they have bought at the store. Then sometimes on a Sunday an old hen from the family flock is served up. Baked beans is a standard dish. Graham flour is largely used in cooking for the sake of economy. Doughnuts ap-pear frequently, and cider apple-sauce is a familiar relish, while pie and tea are apt to be regarded as essentials at each meal. In the more prosperous families, when the people are not penurious, and the housewife is intelligent and a good cook, the fare, though in many ways still simple, is yet so varied and good and well-served that it is thoroughly enjoyable to any one not chronically cross-grained and dyspeptic. The hill country itself, with all its rugged-ness, is charming; and it has made a grand record in the men and women that have gone forth from its rocky farms. True there are plenty more who still long to go. It is not at all certain they would gain by it. For, as Thackeray says in the final sentences of "Vanity Fair," "Which of us has his desire, or, having it, is satisfied?"